THE YOUNG WIDOW

AN AMBITION & DESTINY NOVEL

VL MCBEATH

The Young Widow
By VL McBeath

Copyright © 2020 by VL McBeath, Valyn Publishing
(a trading company of Valyn Ltd).

For more about this author please visit:
https://vlmcbeath.com

*

Editing services provided by Susan Cunningham
(www.perfectproseservices.com)
Cover design by Michelle Abrahall
(www.michelleabrahall.com)

ISBNs:

978-1-9161340-6-5 (Kindle Edition)
978-1-9161340-7-2 (Paperback)

Main category - FICTION / Historical
Other category - FICTION / Sagas

NOTICES

The Young Widow is a standalone novel. Chapter 1 links into a scene at the end of Chapter 23 of *Hooks & Eyes* (Part 1 of The *Ambition & Destiny* Series); however, it is not necessary to have read the full series to enjoy this book.

This story was inspired by real life events but as it took place over two hundred years ago, parts of the storyline and all characterisation is fictitious. Names have been changed and any resemblance to real persons, living or dead, is purely coincidental.

CHAPTER ONE

Great Barr, Staffordshire. 27th December 1848

I t had been a pleasant Christmas. One of the best, Ann would say, although she had to admit it hadn't been without its problems. The joy on her grandson's face when he learned that Mr Wetherby had proposed marriage to Mary, his mother, would warm her heart for years to come, although sadly it hadn't had the same impression on the boy's mother. No, her daughter-in-law, if she could still call her that, had been distracted when she'd arrived four days earlier and nothing had cheered her since.

Ann took a sip from the cup of tea cooling on the dining table and glanced across to Mary.

"You're quiet this morning. Are you still thinking about the marriage proposal?"

Mary sighed and put her knitting down in front of her. "I am. I thought I'd made my mind up last night, but now I'm not so sure. I want to feel happy about it but I can't."

1

"Don't you think you'll be happy if you accept?"

Mary's eyes filled with tears. "How can I be? I'd be marrying him for all the wrong reasons."

Ann pursed her lips. "Staying on your own won't bring Charles back and you need to do what's best for the children."

"I know and I think Mr Wetherby will be good with them. That's why it's so hard. I just hope that if I say yes, it's the right decision." Mary's hands twisted together on her lap.

"I'm sure it will be. From what Martha's said I believe he's a lovely man who thinks the world of you, not to mention William and Mary-Ann. Men like that don't come around very often. You should take the chance when you can."

"It's just that I can't forget Charles..."

Ann turned around to check that no one was on the stairs behind her and then stood up to close the dining room door. "Can I tell you a story? Very few people know this, because they've no need to, but before I met Pa, I was a widow."

Mary's eyes widened. "Surely not, you and Pa have been married forever."

Ann chuckled. "We have that; forty years it was earlier this month. I was twenty-one and he was twenty-six, but before we met, I'd already been married. I was only eighteen when my father walked me up the aisle, but two years later, my husband succumbed to consumption. Fortunately, we'd had no children."

Ann saw the sympathy in Mary's eyes. "Don't be sorry for me. In many ways it was the best thing that could have happened, although it didn't feel that way at the time."

"But you understand what I've been going through? Is that why you've been so good to me? Because your husband's family were good to you?"

Ann shook her head. "No, not exactly." Her eyes glazed over as she thought back to the day of her young husband's funeral. It was the start of a year she would never forget...

CHAPTER TWO

London, January 1808

Ann stood by the open grave fighting to hold back her tears. Her mother had been right; she never should have come. 'There are reasons women don't go to the graveside,' she had said, 'and tears are one of them. Showing your emotions in front of so many men is most undignified. Don't expect me to come with you.'

For the first time in her life, Ann had disobeyed her mother. It may not be usual for women to go the graveside, but what else could she do? Thomas had been her husband, and despite the fact she had only married him at her father's bidding, she was the only family he had left. She couldn't let him make this final journey alone; although what she was doing to her reputation by being here, she daren't think. She bit down on her bottom lip and bowed her head over the grave. All she wanted to do was say farewell, to thank him for taking care of her. Was that so wrong? Wiping her eyes with the handkerchief she held discreetly in her right hand, she straightened her back and held her head high.

Father Jacobs broke her concentration by throwing a piece of earth onto the coffin. She glanced across the grave to see the heavy-set man hunched over his Book of Common Prayer, the black robe he wore over his suit flapping in the icy breeze. She shivered as she stared at the book, the burial pages well defined from years of overuse.

"Foreasmuch as it hath pleased Almighty God of his great mercy to take unto himself the soul of our dear brother here departed..."

He indicated for her to toss the pile of earth she was clutching, onto the coffin.

"We therefore commit his body to the ground; earth to earth, ashes to ashes, dust to dust; in sure and certain hope of the Resurrection to eternal life..."

The tears now welling in her eyes were suddenly tears of anger rather than grief. She was a God-fearing woman; why had the Lord chosen to punish her so harshly? She was a mere child, not yet twenty-one, and had married young to appease her father's need to see her settled before he breathed his last. Was that really a sin?

With a final prayer, Father Jacobs finished the service and gestured for her to walk with him.

"I presume you've returned to your mother's house, Mrs Evans." His words were more of a statement than a question and Ann nodded.

"The solicitor will be waiting for us when we get back to the church. He'll read your late husband's Last Will and Testament to you."

Ann breathed a sigh of relief as she realised someone

would read the document to her. Never having been to a funeral before, it hadn't crossed her mind that the reading of the will had any purpose other than showing the intellect of the solicitor. Now she realised it was for the benefit of people like her who weren't important enough to go to school. At least that was something.

The light inside the church came from only half a dozen candles and Ann blinked several times to adjust her eyes to the dark before realising there was a man in front of the altar at the far end of the church. He stood up and offered Ann his hand as she approached.

"Mrs Evans, please take a seat. May I offer my condolences? I'm Mr Wood and I'm here representing Wood and Sons, your late husband's solicitors. I have some news that I hope will make today's events slightly more bearable."

As she sat down, Ann didn't miss the look that passed between the solicitor and the priest.

"Now, let me begin. As your late husband's parents and his elder brother have already gone to meet their Lord, you become the principal beneficiary of his will. Were you aware of that?"

"He had mentioned it." The cavernous body of the church swallowed Ann's whisper.

"But I believe you have no father to oversee the estate for you?"

"No."

The solicitor's lips twisted into a smile. "Well, let me tell you that Wood and Sons are the executors of the will and we're only too happy to manage the legacy your husband left you."

"He's left me a legacy?"

"He has indeed, Mrs Evans. Now, let me start at the beginning." The solicitor unfurled a sheet of parchment. "This is the Last Will and Testament of Mr Thomas Evans Esquire, late of St John Street, Clerkenwell, dated February 11, 1807."

Ann couldn't stop her mind from wandering as the solicitor detailed Thomas's personal effects and the ideas he'd had for them. Given he was a man of few possessions, it wouldn't take her long to deal with them.

"Mrs Evans, are you listening?"

"Yes, I'm sorry, I was thinking about what you were saying. Please, go on."

"Upon my death, I leave the sum of twenty pounds to my wife Mrs Ann Evans for her exclusive use to provide a roof over her head."

"Twenty pounds?" Ann's eyes were wide. "I'd no idea he had that much."

The solicitor pursed his lips. "As I'm sure you're aware, Mr Evans senior was the owner of a successful import and export company in Bristol. Upon his death, your husband inherited a significant proportion of that business, not to mention his father's personal effects. Now, may I continue?"

Ann's cheeks burned as she nodded. *Why didn't Thomas tell me?*

Mr Wood returned to the parchment. "Of the remainder of my estate, once all debts and funeral expenses have been settled, I instruct my executors to sell all outstanding assets and place the money into trust to provide for my wife, the said Mrs Ann Evans. From this she should receive an annual income of fifty pounds to be paid by four quarterly instalments, until such time that she remarries."

Ann stared at the solicitor. "He's leaving me fifty pounds a year?"

"Indeed."

Her head was spinning. "But only until I remarry. What happens then? Will I lose it…?"

The smile disappeared from the solicitor's face. "*If* you remarry? I would suggest you're not too hasty about that. You're a woman of means now."

Ann shivered as a muscle in the solicitor's jaw twitched. "But what if I want to?"

The solicitor breathed deeply through his nose. "If you must remarry, you'll be free to withdraw the money from the trust to do with as you will."

She sat back in her chair her eyes not leaving the solicitor. "C-can I ask … how much that will be?"

"I'm sure you needn't worry yourself with such details. It's terribly complicated… We have expenses to deduct and suchlike, and it could be years before you're eligible to withdraw it. My father and I will deal with it for you…"

Ann could feel her cheeks getting hotter. "Yes, I'm sure you can, but could you give me an idea?"

Father Jacobs patted her hand. "A rough estimate, if you wouldn't mind, Mr Wood. How much will you be investing?"

The solicitor flicked through the papers in front of him. "Well, I can't say with certainty but if you must know, once all property and other assets are sold it is likely to be of the order of five hundred pounds."

"Five hundred pounds! Oh, my goodness." Ann swayed in her chair, gripping the edge of the table for support.

The solicitor curled his lip. "Precisely, madam. Your husband realised it would be too much for you to deal with, which is why he named us as executors. We'll take good care of it, for a small fee, of course."

"Yes, of course." Ann paused, concentrating on her breathing while her head cleared. "Well, thank you. I'm sure I couldn't manage it on my own."

Once the formalities were over, Father Jacobs stood up and helped Ann from her seat.

"Would you like me to escort you home?"

Ann smiled. "That would be most kind. I fear I've had such a shock that my legs may struggle to carry me."

"You're a very fortunate young lady," the priest said as they stepped into the low winter sun.

"Fortunate?" Ann put a hand to her mouth when she realised how indelicate her tone sounded. "I'm sorry, Father, but I'm only twenty years old and yet I'm a widow. How can you consider me fortunate?"

The priest offered her his arm. "Unfortunately, Mrs Evans, you're not unusual in being widowed so young. You are, however, fortunate that your husband left such a substantial amount of money for your future."

Despite the chill in the air, Ann's cheeks flushed. "Yes, you're right. Forgive me, I misunderstood."

The priest patted her hand. "All is forgiven, my child, but I mentioned the money as something of a warning to you. If word gets around that you're the custodian of such a large amount, it could make you an attractive catch for any number of scoundrels wanting your hand in marriage. I'm afraid to say that you must trust nobody. The love of money has a terrible power to corrupt."

Ann gasped. "I hadn't thought of that."

"You're still young, my dear, but might I suggest you keep

word of your inheritance between yourself and Mrs Davies ... your mother. I won't breathe a word about it."

"Thank you for the warning, Father." Ann paused. "I can see this legacy will have an impact in ways I can't imagine. I promise I won't tell a soul."

"There might be another problem though." The priest hesitated before continuing. "I imagine you'll want to pay a tithe to the church?"

"Well, yes ... if you think I should." The thought hadn't crossed her mind.

The priest patted her hand again. "I understand this is all new to you but the thing is, if you give too much money all at once, people will notice."

Ann peered at him. "So you mean I shouldn't give any?"

A twisted smile crossed the priest's face. "Not quite. I suggest you continue with your usual offering when you come to church, but we make a private arrangement about the rest. Nobody else need know."

"I-if you say so ... although it could be weeks before I get any money."

"I'm sure I can wait."

A shiver ran down Ann's spine as the priest patted her hand. "Actually, Father, would you mind if I walked the rest of the way on my own? I'm feeling much better, now. Good day to you."

Within minutes, Ann approached the small terraced house she shared with her mother and two sisters, grateful that the activity in the street had quietened down while she'd been out. Most mornings, there was a steady procession of cattle and sheep as herders drove them past their doorstep towards Smithfield market, but as with every Monday, today was market day, and there was barely enough room for them to pass. Now all that was left were mounds of filth that covered the road and there was no way of avoiding it. Covering her nose with the collar of her cloak, she picked her way across the road and trudged up the steps to the front door. After stopping to remove her shoes, she stepped indoors but she hadn't taken off her cloak before her mother was upon her.

"Where on earth have you been? You've still got the front step to scrub and those potatoes won't peel themselves. I can't do everything myself while you're swanning off, making a fool of yourself."

Ann stared at the steely face of her mother. The jet black hair she wore in a knot at the nape of her neck was devoid of even the slightest curl and did nothing to soften the angular features of her face. Ann shuddered at the thunderous look in her eyes. "No, I'm sorry, I'll do it now." She retrieved her shoes before hurrying into the scullery, tears stinging her eyes. *Couldn't she be nice to me, just this once?*

"And another thing..." Her mother had followed her. "We're going through too much coal since you came back. One shovelful at a time."

"It's been cold..."

"Not that cold, it hasn't. Now, get a move on."

Ann bit down on her lower lip and squeezed her eyes shut. *Perhaps you could do them instead of expecting me to do everything.* She stood by the sink waiting for her mother to disappear back into the living room. How she would love to stand up to her, but she knew she never would. With a deep sigh, she picked up the bucket and scrubbing brush and headed into the back yard for some water. It was full of children but there were only two women waiting for the tap. *Maybe if I tell her about the money, it'll put a smile on her face.* Seconds later she gave an involuntary shake of the head. *She'll only want it from me. She'll say I'm too young to have so much. No, Mr Wood can take care of it. She needn't know anything about it ... not yet anyway.*

CHAPTER THREE

Four o'clock in the afternoon. It was a time of day Ann had grown to hate. Most respectable ladies would be taking afternoon tea, but since she had moved back in with her mother, it was the time she scrubbed the front doorstep. The dirty, disgusting doorstep that never seemed to be free from the filth of the livestock. Not for the first time, she thought of the nineteen gold sovereigns that now lay hidden under a floorboard in the bedroom. *I shouldn't be working as a maid.*

With a glance up at the darkening sky, she bent down to pick up the bucket from under the tap. The shorter days of winter may be waning and the ice on the inside of the windows had finally disappeared, but that didn't mean it was warm. There was still a biting wind howling around the back yard, and she imagined it would be worse on the front.

With a sigh, she walked through the ginnel into the street and crouched down before plunging the scrubbing brush into the freezing water. She'd need to work quickly if her hand wasn't to get frostbite. The sound of the bristles scratching the stone steps drowned out most of the chaos on the street behind her, but it was no consolation. She'd wager the noise of the streets wouldn't worry the ladies in their drawing rooms.

"You've got your work cut out there."

Ann jumped as a man spoke from behind her. "I beg your pardon?" She scrambled to her feet and backed towards the house, wiping her hands on the apron she wore over her coat.

The man raised his hat. "Forgive me, I shouldn't have startled you."

She twisted the apron in her fingers. "Can I help?"

The stranger stood taller than most gentleman and his dishevelled curly brown hair set him apart from the fashionable young men of the City. He glanced down the street where a succession of narrow houses were interspersed with coaching inns. "It must be a difficult place to keep clean, especially on a day like today. I've never seen so many animals being herded to market down a single street before. I imagine the mistress of the house is glad she has you to do the dirty work."

Ann flinched before glancing back at the house. "I-I suppose she is."

The stranger studied her, his dark eyes sparkling as he held her gaze. "I'm sorry if I disturbed you, but you looked like you needed a little company. Sometimes it helps to wear a smile."

Ann lowered her eyes. "Perhaps it isn't always appropriate."

"No, I don't suppose it is. I'm sorry, I shouldn't have been so forward. I'm new to London and haven't learned the ways yet. When you live in the countryside, as I normally do, you don't have to worry about such things."

Ann kicked at a loose stone on the ground. What could she say? Her mother would be furious if she saw her talking to a strange man, especially so soon after going to the burial of her husband. Perhaps she should have worn her mourning clothes for longer.

"I'll be off then." The stranger raised his hat once more but hesitated. "I don't want you to get into trouble for talking to a stranger, so let me introduce myself. I'm Mr Charles Jackson, Chas for short, a brassfounder from Birmingham. I'm spending a few months with my uncle, Mr George Jackson. You may know him. He lives around the corner."

Ann shook her head. "No, I'm afraid I don't, but there should be work for you around here."

Mr Jackson grimaced. "That's what I'm hoping, Miss...?"

Ann stared at the ground. "Evans ... Mrs Evans."

Mrs...?

Mr Jackson had said nothing, but he didn't need to. Ann could see the confusion in his eyes.

"I'm a widow." The words were out of her mouth before she thought about them.

It was Mr Jackson's turn to nod. "I'm sorry. Now I understand about the smile. You have my condolences but I really must be going. It was nice to meet you, Mrs Evans."

Ann watched as he hurried from her and turned left into Compton Street, the first junction he came to. *Is this to be my fate? To remain unloved and unloveable because I'm a widow?* Tears sprang unbidden to her eyes and she angrily brushed them away.

"What are you doing out there? You should have finished that step by now." Ann could feel her mother's eyes boring into the back of her and they fixed her feet to the spot. *How long has she been there?* A cold chill ran down her spine before she breathed a sigh of relief. *Not long enough, she'd have said something by now.*

"Come along, what are you waiting for?"

"I'm coming." Ann stooped down to pick up her bucket before throwing the dirty water into the road. "I just need to get some clean water to rinse it."

With a nod, her mother turned back into the house, but Ann couldn't move. She stood and let her gaze rest on the street corner that apparently led to Mr Jackson's residence. *What's a respectable gentleman like him doing talking to someone he mistook for a maid?* And what was she thinking telling him she was a widow? Had she lost all sense of respectability? *Please Lord, don't let Mother have seen us.*

Try as she might, Ann couldn't find sleep that night. Being in the same room as her sisters wasn't as easy as it had been before she married but at least she had a bed to herself. She glanced across the room to the bed opposite. Jane was only two years younger than her, but now shared her bed with their younger sister, Susan. She was only ten years old and often became agitated during the night, something that disturbed Jane and caused Ann no end of guilt. On top of that, it sounded like her mother had had a glass of gin too many and the rumble of snoring carried from the bedroom she had to herself at the back of the house. Ann put her head under the blankets to dull the sound. *I don't suppose they're any happier about me being here than I am.*

For the short duration of her marriage to Thomas, they had rented a room in a house several doors down. He'd been promising to buy a property in the area and had rented somewhere while he looked for something suitable. It wasn't the same as having a house of their own but at least it had given them time alone, something she never got now. *If only I could get a room for myself again. It would help us all out, and I've got the money...* But her mother would ask where it had come from and how much there was. She shuddered. Why had Thomas insisted on selling his father's property and putting the money into trust rather than leaving it to her? She didn't need the money, she couldn't buy anything of substance in her own right, but she could have managed if she'd been left a house, even if it was in Bristol. She sighed. Thomas must have thought he was doing the right thing. Still, it would have been nice.

Perhaps she needed to go far away, to a place her mother wouldn't find her. Where was that place Mr Jackson had mentioned? Birmingham? She seemed to remember hearing about it when she was in Bristol but had no idea where it was. Presumably it was miles away. Perhaps she could start a new life there, even take off her wedding ring and pretend she'd never married. A smile flicked across her lips. Dare she hope that Mr Jackson might stop and talk to her again? She could ask him how to get there and where she should stay. She had enough money for a stagecoach.

A cry from the bed on the opposite wall broke her thoughts.

"Susan?" Ann sat up in bed. The nightlight in the holder on the wall flickered onto the bed showing her young sister tossing and turning. Thankfully, within seconds the noise subsided. *It must be another bad dream.* Relieved she didn't have to step onto the cold floor, she lay back down again. *I can't walk out on them.* If I'm not here, Mother will only take it out on them. They managed when I was only a few doors away, they could visit me if they wanted to get away, but if I take a stagecoach...

Tears once again filled her eyes and ran down the side of her face onto the lumpy pillow beneath. Was there to be no way out?

CHAPTER FOUR

Mrs Davies was washing the breakfast dishes in the scullery when Ann found her. She didn't turn around as Ann fastened her cloak around her neck and reached for her basket.

"I'll be going then."

"You should have gone half an hour ago, all the cheap cuts of meat'll be gone."

Ann pursed her lips and studied the back of her mother's faded dress. They weren't exactly poor, but her mother refused to spend money on clothes when she had to put food on the table. She glanced down at her own dress. It was time she had a new one too, but she couldn't buy one without telling her mother where she'd got the money from. And she wasn't ready for that.

"I'm sure I'll find something." Ann was turning to leave when Mrs Davies finally stopped to speak to her.

"And don't be out long. We need to give all the blankets a good beating while it's dry and I'm not doing them myself."

"I'm sure Jane can help you; I'll see you later." Ann wasn't proud of herself for adding another chore to her sister's list, but she needed to get away, for an hour at least. She pulled the front door closed behind her and held her breath. It was market day again and the smell from the droves of livestock was overpowering. She should be used to it by now. Still, it was a small price to pay to have some time to herself. She squinted up at the sun as it peeped out from behind the clouds. She'd take as long as she needed and be back when she was good and ready.

She reached the junction of Compton Street and paused, wondering if Mr Jackson lived in one of the finer houses at the far end. They were bigger than those on St John Street, and she imagined almost all had maids. *I don't suppose any of the ladies down there would scrub their own steps.* With a final perusal of the street, she continued on, waiting for the cattle to pass before she turned off and headed towards Clerkenwell Green. Not that there was any green to be seen. The stalls were set out in a square around the central well, while the horses and carts that had brought in the goods stood nearby impeding the way of those shopping. Ann sighed. Was the whole of Clerkenwell out this morning? Holding her basket close, she pushed her way through the crowd to her usual stalls.

"Mornin', miss." A costermonger was waiting for an order at the grocery barrow next to her usual butcher's. "What will it be?"

Ann eyed the vegetables before her.

"We've some nice cabbages left."

"Yes, thank you. I'll take one, and a couple of carrots. That should be enough for today." She was eyeing the meat on the stall next to her when the owner stepped forward and gave her a cheery grin, his bushy sideburns almost joining up with his lips as he did.

"Mornin', Mrs Evans. I've saved a nice piece of ham for you."

A smile crossed her face as she handed over a penny for her vegetables. *At least that will prove Mother wrong.*

With her change back in her purse she walked to where the butcher held out a small joint. "How's that for you?"

"I'm sure it will be very nice. How much is that?"

"For you, thruppence." He wrapped the meat in some newspaper as she rummaged in her purse. "You've got a bit more colour in your cheeks this mornin', if you don't mind me saying. Not that I blame you for being peaky these last few weeks. Terrible business it was with Mr Evans, and him not even thirty. Not much older than me, as it happens. Nasty thing, consumption. If you ever need a man for anything, you know where I am."

"Thank you, Mr Williams. I'm sure that's very kind." She picked up the meat. "Good day to you."

"Goodbye, then. See you tomorrow."

Feeling Mr Williams's eyes following her, Ann jostled her way back through the crowds and headed for the main road. The street was still busy when she arrived and she waited for a gap in the livestock before attempting to cross. Seeing her chance, she stepped off the footpath just as a horse and carriage pulled out in front of her. She fell backwards, but as she did, a hand caught hold of her, plucking her to safety.

"Be careful there, miss. Good gracious, it's Mrs Evans, isn't it?"

Ann's heart skipped a beat as she looked up to see a pair of deep brown eyes staring down at her. "My, Mr Jackson. What are you doing here?"

"I could ask the same of you."

Ann's brow furrowed. "I-I've been to market to get something for dinner. I usually come around this time."

It was Mr Jackson's turn to frown. "I wasn't aware that was a job for a general maid. We usually let Cook do that sort of thing."

Ann stood paralysed. *Do I tell him I'm not a maid? What if it embarrasses him?*

Concern crossed Mr Jackson's face. "I'm sorry, I didn't mean to insult you. I'm sure you're only doing your job."

"No ... no, I'm not." Ann's voice squeaked as she spoke.

"You mean you shouldn't be here? Is that why you look so frightened?" He grinned as he tapped the side of his nose. "Don't worry, I won't say anything."

"No. It's not that." Ann took a deep breath. "I'm not a maid."

Mr Jackson's brows pulled together. "But you were cleaning the step..."

Despite the cold, Ann felt her cheeks burning. "It's my mother's house, but we don't have a maid. I help out with the chores."

Mr Jackson took off his hat and bowed. "Please forgive me, I'm clearly a numbskull." He looked her up and down. "I can't say I'm surprised. I thought you were rather well dressed for a maid."

Ann pulled her cloak more tightly around her to hide her dowdy grey dress. "Really?"

Mr Jackson's eyes glimmered. "Really. Tell me, are you about to walk back up St John Street?"

"Y-yes. Why?" Ann's heart fluttered as she noticed the dimples in Mr Jackson's cheeks.

"I'm going that way myself. May I escort you?"

Ann's eyes flicked around the nearby crowd. "Well ... I'm not sure. What will people think?"

Mr Jackson shrugged. "I don't suppose they'll think anything."

She chewed on her lip as she played with the handle of her basket. *What am I thinking? I'm a widow who buried her husband no more than a month ago. But it's only like having a chaperone; we're not going to be alone together.* Finally, a smile settled on her face. "Yes, you may. I'd enjoy the company."

"Splendid." That glint was back in his eyes. "May I take your basket? It looks heavy."

"Oh no, really it isn't. It's just the cabbage, it takes up so much room."

"Well, let me help you anyway." Mr Jackson took her basket and ushered her around some cattle.

"Is this what it's like in the country?" Ann asked as they reached the far side of the road.

"Not really, although we're not without livestock, obviously. Our markets are small compared with the one you have here. In Birmingham, I would say there are no more than three dozen cattle, even on a busy day."

Ann giggled. "I didn't mean that, I meant do you have market stalls like this?"

"Oh yes, although again not as big as this one. There are nowhere near as many people in Birmingham as there are down here."

"Really?"

"Why does that surprise you? You don't sound as if you're from these parts yourself."

"Can you tell?"

"I couldn't say where you do come from only that it's not from around here. Are you going to tell me?"

Ann's cheeks flushed. "I'm from Bristol originally, but I've been in London for nearly three years."

"Ah, hence the surprise about the size of Birmingham. Bristol was a big port in its day. I imagine it was busy."

Ann nodded. "It was. I wasn't allowed to go to the docks even with my mother; it was only suitable for men, unless there was good reason."

"Did your father work on the docks?"

Ann hesitated. *How many more questions is he going to ask?* "Yes."

"I suppose he moved to London when the trade in Bristol started to dwindle."

How does he know that? "Were you acquainted with my father?"

"Were?" Mr Jackson's eyes narrowed.

Ann lowered her head. "He died a couple of years ago, not long after we moved here. He caught influenza..."

"Well then, I can't say I did. I am sorry though. You seem to have had too much sadness for such a short life."

Ann shrugged. "Doesn't everyone?"

Mr Jackson's eyes glazed over. "I suppose so."

He remained in a trance, and Ann gave a small cough to distract him. "If you didn't meet my father, how did you know why we moved to London?"

The glint returned to Mr Jackson's eyes. "It's been in the newspapers, of course. Once the rumours started that the trade in slaves was being abolished, everyone knew ports like Bristol would suffer. And so it's proved."

Ann's shoulders relaxed. "So, what brought you to London?"

"Me? It's a lot bigger than Birmingham and there's more work down here."

"Is there no work in Birmingham for a brassfounder?"

Mr Jackson's mouth twisted. "Not enough, it would seem." His pace quickened and Ann scampered to keep up with him.

"I'm sorry, I shouldn't have asked. I've never been to the country and so I've no idea what it's like. I didn't mean to pry."

Mr Jackson slowed his pace. "No, I'm sorry, how would you know?"

A crease remained on Ann's forehead. "Would you mind if I asked another question?"

Mr Jackson studied her. "It depends what it is."

"It's nothing really, but do men and women usually talk to each other without chaperones?"

Ann relaxed once more when Mr Jackson laughed.

"Oh, all the time. Didn't you do that in Bristol? I thought it was only London that had all these silly rules."

"I don't remember, I was too young for it to matter when we were in Bristol."

"And I suppose you married before you knew much about it."

Ann stared at him, her mouth open. As soon as she realised, she closed it quickly. "How did you know that?"

Mr Jackson shook his head. "My dear Mrs Evans. You're still little more than a child, and so I imagine you must have married at a young age to be a widow already. Was it a marriage of convenience?"

"No, it wasn't!"

Mr Jackson shrugged. "I just wondered if your father had wanted something. I imagine you'd have made a rather splendid bargaining tool."

"What a terrible thing to say." Ann's cheeks were burning. "He did no such thing; he wanted what was best for me."

"Which was to marry the son of an acquaintance?"

Ann stopped in her tracks but Mr Jackson only raised an eyebrow at her.

"They were friends!" Ann's heart sank as Mr Jackson continued up the road. She'd never shouted at a man before and by the looks of it, it was something he wasn't used to.

"Mr Jackson, stop, please. I'm sorry. I didn't mean to raise my voice. You just seem to know so much about me and, well ... it doesn't feel right."

"I know nothing about you, Mrs Evans, but I've seen this sort of thing before."

Ann held his gaze but couldn't read his expression.

"Maybe your father did what he thought was best. I'm sorry. Shall we continue?"

They walked the rest of the way in silence until they reached the corner of Compton Street.

"I'll take my basket now, thank you." Ann reached for it but Mr Jackson held it away.

"Nonsense. What sort of man offers to walk a lady home only to take himself home instead? Let me walk you to the door."

"No, please, there's no need." Ann's voice squeaked as she spoke. "It's not far."

Mr Jackson cocked his head to one side. "Aren't I good enough to be seen with you?"

"Of course you are, but it's my mother. She ... well, let's just say she wouldn't understand the ways of the countryside."

Mr Jackson's face was stern as he nodded. "Very well. I don't want to get you into trouble." He handed her the basket but kept hold of the handle as she tried to take it.

"Would you object to me walking you home from the market if we meet there again?"

Ann's heart skipped a beat. "No, I don't suppose I would."

The corners of his mouth turned up. "Splendid. I shall watch out for you."

With her heart racing, Ann wrested the basket from him and somehow found the strength to put one foot in front of the other as she continued on her way. She could feel his eyes still on her back, but she daren't look around. She might never make it home if she did.

As she reached the front doorstep, she allowed herself a glance back down the road but Mr Jackson had turned to leave. She stared at the spot where he'd stood. *What was he even doing at the market? He never did tell me.*

CHAPTER FIVE

Ann was up early the following morning. If Mr Jackson was walking down St John Street on the way to work, she may see him again. Only she had to be more confident this time. He was obviously used to talking to women, and she needed to be ready for that.

"What are you doing up so early?" Her mother joined her in the living room as she fastened her cloak.

Ann shrugged. "You were right yesterday when you said I was too late for the best cuts of cheap meat, so I thought I'd go earlier today."

"You brought home a nice piece of ham."

Ann's cheeks coloured. "That was fortunate. Mr Williams had put it to one side for another customer, but they didn't want it. I turned up at the right time."

"You should ask him to put something away for you every day if it saves you going out so early. It's not even light yet."

Ann studied the floor. "As much as I might like to, I'm sure I can't do that. Now if you'll excuse me, I must be going."

The first shafts of sunlight were breaking over the

irregularly shaped rooftops as Ann stepped out of the house, but the wind still held an icy chill and she pulled her cloak tightly around her. At least winter was nearly over, only another couple of weeks for her to get out of bed in the dark.

With her head down into the wind she made her way to the corner of Compton Street where she paused. *Where is he?* She squinted into the distance, but her shoulders drooped. *That was a waste of time getting out of bed so early.*

With a sigh, she continued towards the market, amazed that by the time she arrived it was already busy. *These people must have been up half the night.* She pretended to look at the stalls of fabric and animal skins before turning the corner towards the meat and vegetables. She gave the produce an occasional glance but barely noticed it. Her eyes were elsewhere as she wondered whether it too early for a gentleman to visit the market. If indeed that was what he'd been doing when he'd saved her. She was much earlier today than she had been; perhaps she was too early. Or maybe he hadn't been to the market at all yesterday but had just been on his way home from the City and had happened to catch hold of her. Ann sighed. No, he was a brassfounder. He wouldn't have been to the City ... unless he was investing some money. Ann paused, recalling the image of Mr Jackson. He'd looked very smart in his breeches and tailcoat ... although she wasn't keen on the hat. She'd tried her best to ignore it, praying it didn't mean he was a dissenter. '*Of course he is.*' The sound of her mother's voice was so vivid that she jumped and turned in a full circle to make sure she was alone. With a shake of her head, she moved towards the next stall. *So, what if he is a Quaker? Doesn't God love all men?* '*He'll never marry you, you know*'. Ann put her hands to her ears.

Stop this. I've met him twice. Why is it so wrong to want to see him again?

Pushing all thoughts of Mr Jackson from her mind, she purposefully strode to the meat stall.

"You have a good selection today." She avoided Mr Williams's gaze as she studied the meat.

"That'll be because you're here so early. Couldn't you sleep?"

Ann forced a smile. "I slept well enough, but I particularly wanted some braising steak this morning."

There was a twinkle in Mr Williams's eyes as he winked at her. "You should have said so yesterday an' I'd have put it to one side for you."

"I'm sure you would, but I don't like to impose. Besides, I only decided last night."

"It's never an imposition for you." He flashed her a broad grin. "Now, is there anything you'd like for tomorrow?"

Ann hurriedly took the meat and offered him a shilling. "No, thank you. Not at the moment."

"Well, if you ever do want anything, you just need to say."

Ann took her change. "Thank you, Mr Williams. Good day."

She hurried away, studying the faces of those around her as she picked up the rest of her shopping. There was no sign of him. Before long she put her head down and headed back towards the main road. He wasn't coming. Perhaps it was for the best. If he really was a dissenter, it would cause no end of trouble with her mother and she couldn't face the arguments. No, it was better this way.

Her basket was heavier than she'd thought, and she struggled back up St John Street alone. She was about to cross over Compton Street when she heard footsteps heading towards her. Unable to resist, she peeked to her right, just as Mr Jackson approached.

"My word. Have you been to market already?" He took out his pocket watch. "It's not half past eight yet."

Ann's confidence left her. "I-I needed an early start. We have things to do at home."

"Well, never mind, let me carry the basket the rest of the way."

Ann pulled it away from him. "No, please don't. Mother wouldn't understand." Her eyes drifted up to his rounded, wide-brimmed hat.

"Ah." Mr Jackson felt the rim of his hat. "Yes, it can cause problems. Does it bother you?"

Ann stared, her mouth opening and closing several times before she found any words. "I-I don't know. Are you really a Quaker?"

He nodded. "My family are."

"Perhaps that explains a few things then ... like why you talk to women so easily."

Mr Jackson shrugged. "Why shouldn't I? Unlike the established church, we believe all people are equal in the eyes of God. White, black, men, women... It doesn't matter."

"Is that why you talk to me?"

Mr Jackson's eyes softened. "I talk to you because I want to. Is there anything wrong with that?"

Ann shook her head. "Not to me, but..."

"But there is to your mother?"

Ann sighed. "She's had a hard time recently. Since Father died, she's had to take care of my younger sisters ... and now I've moved back, too." Ann paused. *Why am I defending her?*

"It can't be easy."

"It's not too bad. Father left her with the house and a bit of money, so we manage well enough."

"And I imagine he thought you'd be well provided for ... marrying you off as he did."

Ann lowered her eyes but tensed as Mr Jackson put a finger under her chin and lifted her face to look at his.

"Don't be sad. Those eyes are too pretty to be full of tears. Such a lovely shade of blue."

Ann brushed them away with the back of her hand. "I'm sorry. I really must be going. Mother will be wondering where I am."

Mr Jackson straightened up. "Very well but tell me, do you usually go to the market so early?"

Ann shook her head. "I-I just couldn't sleep last night, so I thought I'd get a good start to the day."

"But perhaps you won't do that every day. If I'm here at this time tomorrow might I have a chance of walking with you?"

The glint in Mr Jackson's eyes was unmistakable and Ann allowed herself a smile. "I would say there's a good chance I'll be here around this time."

"Splendid." He studied the tall, thin buildings around them. "This is an excellent place to stop and read the newspaper ... as long as there are not too many cattle passing. It's good for the constitution to stand when you're reading, did you know that?"

Ann giggled as she shook her head. "I don't think I did." *Not that I'd ever stand to read ... or sit for that matter.* "Perhaps I'll see you tomorrow then."

She would have skipped the rest of the way home had she

not been worried about what the neighbours would think. By the time she arrived she couldn't take the grin from her face.

"What have you got to look so happy about?" Her mother was watching out for her from the front doorstep.

"Nothing, it's just a lovely day ... the sort of day that makes you think about making a new start."

Her mother's eyes narrowed. "What are you up to?"

"I'm not up to anything, but you must admit, the beginning of spring is something to savour. Think of the warmer days ahead."

"Which only makes the smell of filth rotting in the streets worse. It wasn't as bad as this when your father bought the house."

Ann fought to suppress a sigh. "Are you ever happy about anything?"

"What is there to be happy about living around here? Animals filling the street all day every day, the dirt and smell they leave behind, thieves and pickpockets no more than a stone's throw away, the constant noise..."

"But we have one of the busiest markets in London on our doorstep."

"Which is the cause of all the problems."

Ann shook her head. "Whatever you say, I won't be miserable on a day like today."

"Well, you can still get upstairs and help Jane with the bedrooms. The mattresses need turning for one thing." Her mother took her basket and disappeared into the scullery. "I'll deal with this."

By the time she reached the top of the stairs, Jane was rolling up the piece of carpet that ran between the beds. She looked up as soon as she heard her.

"Where've you been?"

"To the market. Why?"

Jane stood up. "I'd planned on coming with you but by the time I arrived downstairs, you'd already gone. What was the hurry?"

Ann stopped in the doorway. "Why did you want to come with me? You never come with me."

Jane shrugged. "I just wanted a change. I'm tired of being in the house all the time doing nothing but cleaning."

Ann walked over to her sister and put an arm around her shoulder. "I know exactly how you feel. Perhaps we could take a walk this afternoon. I don't suppose Mother will want us to both disappear for the shopping, but if we're quick with our chores, maybe we could find time later."

"I suppose you're right." A weak smile lit up Jane's pale face. "What would I do without you? I'm so glad you're back."

"You managed when I left last time ... and you have Susan. Where is she now?"

"Out in the yard, I think. Mother had her doing the washing."

Ann shook her head. "I'm not surprised she's been having bad dreams. She's ten years old. She shouldn't be doing the washing by herself."

"Do you want to add it to your list of chores? I'm sure I don't."

Ann ran a hand down the side of her head until it reached the chignon she wore on the back of her head. "Not really, but I'll go and see her. She needs some help."

Ann was exhausted by the time she fell into bed that night. She glanced across at Jane and Susan, who were already breathing deeply in the bed opposite. *Bless them, they don't deserve this.* She thought back to her own childhood. Her father had been alive then, and they had two maids who did all the manual work. But everything had changed with his illness. That had been nearly three years ago, and Susan didn't remember any different. *I need to do something. Perhaps Mr Jackson can help.* A smile spread across her face at the thought of meeting him again. *And at least I won't need to get out of bed so early in the morning.*

Despite her weariness, Ann hardly slept a wink. As the hours ticked by, she grew impatient to get up and fix her hair. She'd already wrapped the front in rags to deepen the curls around her face, but they needed brushing out. Not that she'd be able to see anything in the dark. She'd have to trust her fingers that everything was in the right place.

As the first glimmer of light crept around the edges of the drapes, she thought about sitting up to arrange her hair. She already knew which bonnet she would wear and so it really was only the curls at the front she needed to get right.

He's seen you before, why does it matter?

Because I want him to like me as much as I like him. Ann's face flushed as she recalled the glint in his eyes as he'd smiled at her. *I think he likes me already.*

But he's a Quaker.

Ann's body sagged into the bed. *Of all the things...*

She lay staring at the ceiling before she sat bolt upright and pulled the rags from her hair. *What if I don't care that he's a Quaker? If we like each other, it's got nothing to do with Mother...* She pulled a brush through her hair, taking care not to spoil each ringlet. *As long as she doesn't know, she's got nothing to worry about.*

By the time the noise in the street threatened to wake Jane

and Susan, Ann tiptoed out of bed and dressed as quickly and quietly as she could. Hearing movement from her mother's bedroom, she crept downstairs and slipped her cloak from the hook in the hall. With a final glance up the stairs, she stepped outside and pulled the door closed behind her. The fact she had made it out of the house without her mother seeing her had to be a good sign.

She saw Mr Jackson on the street corner before he saw her. He was as dashing as she remembered and looked very sophisticated as he leaned against the wall, the newspaper folded so he could hold it in one hand. Suddenly, she gasped. He was wearing a top hat. It was only yesterday he'd told her he was a Quaker. Would he pretend otherwise for her?

A thrill coursed down her spine and she straightened her back, holding her head high as she walked towards him.

"Good morning, Mr Jackson."

His eyes swept over her as she approached. "Good morning, Mrs Evans. You're looking very pretty today. Is that a new bonnet?"

Ann touched the side of her hat. "Not especially, but it is one of my best. I don't like to keep it just for Sundays."

"Well, I'm very glad you don't, given that I'm unlikely to see you in church."

Ann's eyes strayed to the top of Mr Jackson's head. "But you've changed your hat."

Mr Jackson chuckled. "My other one obviously unsettled you and I didn't like that. Besides, what difference does a hat make?"

Ann cocked her head to one side. "None, I don't suppose, but thank you for being thoughtful. It will make things easier if Mother should see us."

"Even if she does, I hope she'd have nothing to complain about." Mr Jackson offered Ann his arm. "May I escort you properly?"

Ann's heart fluttered as she stared at his arm.

"You've no need to be nervous." Mr Jackson took hold of her hand as she slipped her arm in his.

"I'm not really but you never know who's watching." Ann scanned the passers-by as they started walking. "I hope no one reports us to Mother. She likes to complain first and then think about it later."

"Stop worrying."

She took a deep breath. "May I ask about your parents? Are they in London, too?"

"No. Father died about ten years ago and Mother's still in Birmingham."

"And is she a Quaker?"

"Oh, very much so, as was my Father. They're both very strict about it."

"So she wouldn't be happy about your hat?"

Mr Jackson laughed. "No, I don't suppose she would, but what she doesn't know..."

"I thought the same thing this morning." Ann held Mr Jackson's gaze as he looked down at her, but with the heat rising in her cheeks, she turned away. "If you're here, does your mother have any other children at home?"

Mr Jackson chuckled. "More than you imagine. I think at the last count there were still six there ... or maybe seven. Most of the girls anyway. My brothers and I are the older ones and we've all moved on."

"Good grief, how many of you are there?"

"Twelve of us survived childhood, but my eldest sister

died last year." Ann saw a moment of sadness in Mr Jackson's eyes. "It was a difficult time, especially for Mother. She relied on her more than we knew."

"I'm sorry."

"Yes, we all were, but you pick yourself up and dust yourself off. That's what Mother always says."

"S-so is that why you came down here? To dust yourself off?"

The corner of his mouth lifted. "You could say that. I needed a fresh start and my uncle's been very generous. Anyway, enough of me and my woes, what have you been doing since yesterday?"

Ann gave a deep sigh. "Nothing exciting."

"It can't be that bad."

Ann grimaced as they waited at the side of the road for a herd of cattle to pass. "You've never met my mother. As soon as Father died, she dismissed the maids and announced that she expected me and my sister to do all the work. It's not so bad for us, we're old enough, but she's got my little sister doing as much as everyone else now and she's only ten. It makes me angry, but you can't talk to her. I wouldn't mind if Father had left us penniless..."

Mr Jackson raised an eyebrow. "Perhaps she's just being careful. The money might have to last her a long time."

"You're right, I'm being selfish. At least we have a roof over our heads and it's ours. There are a lot worse off."

"Well, we're a right cheery pair this morning, aren't we?" Mr Jackson grinned at her.

Ann's lips curled upwards. "Perhaps we shouldn't talk about such things. Why don't you tell me about your work?

You're very well dressed for a brassfounder. Are you the boss?"

"Not at the moment." Mr Jackson's face hardened. "Thanks to my uncle, I have no need of a job and so I'm having a splendid time acquainting myself with London. Perhaps you could accompany me when you have time."

Ann's smile grew. "Really? I'd like that. I've not travelled much further than Clerkenwell, but I hear there's much more to the place than that."

"There is indeed. I took a stroll along the banks of the river yesterday and it was very pleasant. Perhaps I can take you on the same walk on Sunday."

"Sunday?" Ann hesitated.

"Do you go to church?"

"Not as such, but … well, my sisters and I often listen to the visiting Methodist preacher on a Sunday afternoon; it's the only time we get to be together…"

Mr Jackson held up his hand. "You don't have to explain. I understand that you don't want to miss your outing."

"I don't … but a walk would be nice." She lowered her eyes, praying he didn't think her too forward.

"Well, we'll have to take it some other time then." They reached the first of the market stalls and stopped. "Why don't you think about it and let me know when would suit you?" His smile was tender. "I'll rearrange my appointments to fit in with you if it means we can spend longer together. Shall I see you at the same time tomorrow?"

CHAPTER SIX

Ann drifted around the market in a daze. *He wants us to walk out together! He'll even change his arrangements to suit me.* Her heart skipped a beat. *I need to speak to Jane.* The idea of listening to a sermon no longer appealed to her. Could she leave Jane and Susan together while she sneaked off? That way she needn't say anything to Mother. No, not Susan. At her age, secrets meant nothing. She'd need an excuse.

Oh my goodness, why is this so hard? I'm a widow, for goodness' sake, I've run my own house. I shouldn't worry about walking out with a new man. In fact, Mother should be pleased I've found someone else. Especially one who has some money. She bit down on her lip as her stomach flipped. *Money. I should have told her about the legacy by now, but when have I had the chance? If she'd shown even one moment of kindness, I would have told her, but if I tell her now, she'll wonder why I kept it a secret. Then what do I say?* She took a deep breath. *If I walk out with Mr Jackson, I can tell her he has money, and that he's been generous. Maybe that will help.* She nodded to herself. *Yes, he can be my generous benefactor.*

"Aren't you stoppin' today, Mrs Evans?"

Ann flinched at the sound of her name and turned to see Mr Williams smiling at her. "Oh, I'm sorry, forgive me. I was in a world of my own."

"That's not like you. Is everything all right?"

"Yes, I'm fine. Now, what do you have today?"

He picked up some neck of lamb and showed it to her.

"Yes, that looks nice." Ann fumbled in her purse for some money.

"Are you sure you're all right?"

"Yes, of course. I-it's just that we've started spring cleaning and there's a lot to think about."

"Well, don't you go doing too much. I worry about a young lass like you."

She took the meat from him and handed him tuppence. "I'm hardly a lass, Mr Williams. I'm a widow if you remember."

"I do remember and my heart bleeds every time I think about it. You're still so young, you need to get yourself another husband."

Ann shivered but forced a smile to stay on her lips as he handed her her change. "All in good time, Mr Williams. Good day to you."

She hurried to the stall behind her and picked up some carrots and potatoes before turning for home. Jane was probably doing the bedrooms, so she'd have a chance to talk to her while Mother was making the bread. *I hope Susan isn't with her.*

The house appeared empty when she arrived home and Ann placed her shopping in the larder before going upstairs.

"Jane, are you there?" She stepped into the bedroom but stopped at the sight of her mother on her hands and knees by the side of the bed. "What are you doing?"

Without a word her mother pulled a money bag from under a floorboard.

"Where did this come from?"

Her mother's voice sent a shiver down her spine. "What are you doing down there? That's private..."

"Not when you're living under my roof expecting free board and lodgings, it's not."

"I'm sorry, please don't shout. I can explain."

"Explain!" Mrs Davies pushed herself to her feet. "You've been hiding nearly twenty pounds in gold sovereigns under the floorboard and you didn't think to mention it? After all I've done for you?"

"I-I was going to tell you ... but I never found the right time." The tears that ran down Ann's face were real.

"Wasn't the time? Father Jacobs said you've had this money for over two months..."

"Father Jacobs! Why would he mention it?"

"Because he's an honest and decent man who can see how I struggle to raise three daughters. You've had ample time to tell me about it, but you've said nothing and let me pay for all the food and coal. Your father's money won't last forever."

"No." Ann wiped her nose with the back of her hand. "I'm sorry. I was hoping to use it to get myself a room. I know I'm a burden to you..."

"A burden. You'd be a lot less of a burden if you

contributed to the housekeeping. I didn't bring you up to tell lies. Well, I'll take this and we'll forget all about it."

"No, it's mine." Ann's voice whined through her tears. "I'll pay you some keep but Thomas left it for me..."

Her mother's dark eyes glared at her before she tipped the coins onto the bed. "It's a little late for that, but let's see what we have here. Father Jacobs said Thomas left you twenty pounds; why's there only eighteen pounds ten shillings and sixpence left?"

"I've been paying my tithe to Father Jacobs. He said I should give two pounds."

"You've been giving money to the church and not me?" Mrs Davies screwed up her face. "Wait until I see Father Jacobs. He has no right to take the money when your family need it."

"He said it was to help the needy."

"In case you haven't noticed, we're needy." Mrs Davies spat out her words. "When did you give it to him? You haven't been to church to put it on the plate since you found these newfangled Methodists."

Ann's cheeks were burning. "He told me not to tell anyone. He said it should be a private donation so nobody would know I had the money."

"So, it's not even gone through the church?"

Ann stepped back as her mother's look became venomous.

"I imagine he's pocketed it himself. I noticed he had a new hat the other day ... I even complimented him on it. Wait 'til I see him."

Ann clung to the door frame for support. "I'm sorry, he told me it was my duty and I thought I could trust him. Why would he lie to me?"

Her mother stood up straight and placed a hand on her heart. "For the love of money is the root of all evil, which while some coveted after, they have erred from the faith, and pierced themselves through with many sorrows." She let her stance relax. "If you knew your Bible, you'd know that."

Ann sank down onto the bed and collected up the money before putting it back in the pouch. "Here, take it. I obviously can't be trusted."

Her mother stared at the pouch but left it where it was. For the first time in years, Ann saw compassion on her face.

"I will take it, but only to save you from yourself. It will still be yours and I'll take a shilling a week to pay for your keep but if you need any for yourself, you must ask. I won't have you giving it away to anyone who tries to take advantage of you."

Ann managed to smile through her tears. "Thank you."

"Well, think on in future."

"I will." She wiped her eyes. "Now's probably a good time to tell you I'll be getting more money from the estate shortly. Thomas set up a legacy leaving me fifty pounds a year, which I'll get a payment from every quarter. I've not had any of that money yet."

The anger on Mrs Davies's face disappeared. "I knew your father was up to something when he insisted you marry Thomas. He wasn't as daft as he looked."

"He wasn't daft at all and I will take care of you, but I'd like to save some money and have my own house one day."

Her mother put an arm around Ann's shoulder. "All in good time, my dear. This changes everything. Perhaps we could even get a maid again."

44

Jane was in the yard hanging out some washing when Ann found her.

"What's the matter with you?" Her sister put the last peg onto the corner of the sheet and turned to face her. "Have you been crying?"

"A bit, but I'll tell you about it later. Will you come for a walk with me this afternoon?"

Jane raised an eyebrow. "Now I know there's something up. We've all the floors to scrub this afternoon."

Ann shook her head. "No, we don't. We're getting a maid to do the heavy duties."

"A maid! She's told you that?"

"If we go out later, I'll tell you about it." Ann's lips curled into a smile. "I've a favour to ask, too."

Jane returned her grin. "I'm sure that if you've got us a maid, I'll be happy to agree to anything."

CHAPTER SEVEN

With the sun now rising earlier than she did in the mornings, Ann strolled down St John Street with a smile on her face. She no longer needed her heavy cloak, and she smoothed down her shorter pelisse to show off more of her new dress. This had become her favourite time of day and she tingled with excitement as she approached Compton Street, where she knew Mr Jackson was waiting for her.

He glanced at his pocket watch as she arrived. "I'd swear we're both arriving earlier each morning."

"It doesn't matter how early I am, you're always waiting for me. How can I rest in bed knowing you're here?" Her heart fluttered as he reached out and touched her fingers. "I wouldn't want to waste our special time."

"I'm sure neither of us would want that." He offered her his arm as they set off towards the market. "As we're early, we may have time for a walk along the river. Would you like that?"

Ann beamed at him. "I would. It seems like such a long

time ago that you first mentioned it and I've been praying for the weather to improve ever since."

"What are we waiting for then? This way." He led her away from Clerkenwell Green down a series of roads to their left. "Doesn't your mother wonder where you go each morning? I'm sure you must spend longer at the market than you used to."

Ann chuckled. "She doesn't seem to notice."

"Isn't that strange? I thought you said she always kept an eye on you."

"She must have got used to me being around and doesn't worry so much. Besides, she's never out of bed when I leave in the morning and so she's no idea how long I've been out."

Mr Jackson snickered. "So that's why you're leaving the house earlier each morning. To avoid her."

Ann's eyes narrowed. "It's as if you can see into my mind. How do you know such things?"

"You forget, I have ... had ... eight sisters. I've seen how they think."

"Well, I'd better watch myself. I'm sure I shouldn't like you to know everything about me, not when I've never had a brother to learn from. You have me at a disadvantage."

"A position I would never abuse." He patted her on the back of the hand. "Come, we'd better get a move on or else we won't see much of the river before we have to turn back."

They walked for over half an hour along the banks of the River Thames before they retraced their steps and headed towards the market. Ann unhooked her arm from his as they reached the first stall, but he caught hold of her hand.

"I thought I'd come with you today ... if you don't mind."

"Of course I don't mind, but I thought you said it wasn't the done thing for a man to be seen shopping."

Mr Jackson's face twisted. "Did I say that? Perhaps I did, but it's quite another matter for a gentleman to accompany his lady to the stalls."

Ann stopped, her mouth open, before she found the words. "Is that what you think I am, your lady?"

He raised an eyebrow. "Don't you think so?"

"Well, yes." Her face broke into a broad smile. "It's just so sudden."

"Sudden! We've been meeting each other every morning for the last two months. I'd hardly call it sudden."

Ann wrinkled her nose at him. "You know what I mean. But what's brought this on?"

Mr Jackson shrugged. "I just wanted our friendship to be more official. There's nothing wrong with that, is there?"

Ann slipped her hand back through his arm. "Nothing at all. Come along, I'll introduce you to Mr Williams the butcher. He's always very friendly."

By the time they arrived at the stalls, the market was busy, and they had to wait in a queue before they reached the meat stall.

"Good morning, Mr Williams." Ann smiled, waiting for him to flash his usual grin, but when it didn't arrive, she removed her arm from Mr Jackson's. "Right, well, what do you have this morning?"

"I've saved you a nice bit of ox tongue." Mr Williams rolled his shoulders, his eyes never leaving Mr Jackson. "You won't get better than this, you won't." He reached under the counter and pulled out the meat.

"No, I must say, it looks very nice, thank you." Ann reached for her purse. "How much is it?"

Mr Williams's gaze finally shifted to Ann. "For anyone else, it would be two shillings, but for you, one shilling and sixpence. I like to keep my special customers happy."

Ann rummaged in her purse and handed him the correct change. "I'm sure that's most kind. Thank you again. Good day."

Mr Jackson put his arm around Ann's back to usher her through the crowd, but when she realised it was no longer there, she turned around to see Mr Williams gripping the top of Mr Jackson's arm.

"You stay away, do you hear me?" Any hint of friendliness on Mr Williams's face had disappeared to be replaced by an expression Ann couldn't fathom. "I'll be watching you."

Without a word, Mr Jackson pulled his arm away and took hold of Ann's hand to lead her through the crowd.

"Are you all right?" he asked once they reached the road. "You've gone very pale."

"Yes, I think so. I'm just surprised at Mr Williams, he's usually most friendly."

Mr Jackson gritted his teeth. "I don't want you seeing him again, do you understand?"

"But what about the meat, I always go there; he's the best butcher in the market and he looks after me."

"I'll bet he does." Mr Jackson stared back towards the stall. "Promise me you'll find somewhere else. I don't want you on your own with him."

Ann's eyes scanned the stalls around her. "Very well. I suppose there are plenty of other places."

With the evenings now light until well after eight o'clock

the temptation to take an evening stroll as well as their morning walk had become irresistible. Unfortunately, the repertoire of excuses Ann used for her mother was running out.

"Where did you say you were tonight?" Mr Jackson asked as the river came into view.

Ann chuckled. "Thankfully, there's a Methodist preacher speaking in the square outside St John's Church. Jane's gone with a few friends and so I said I was with them."

Mr Jackson's face hardened. "Don't you think it's about time you told her the truth?"

She sighed as a chill ran down her spine. "I just know she won't be happy."

"But you can't put it off forever."

"Maybe not, but we had an argument a couple of months ago and since then she's been very pleasant. I don't want to upset her."

"Do you think I'm so bad she'll dislike me before she even meets me?"

"I can't be sure, but I worry about you being a Quaker ... even if you no longer wear the hat. And..."

"And what?"

Ann shrank back under his gaze. "Maybe I'm imagining it, but I've a feeling she doesn't want me to meet anyone else."

"Why on earth wouldn't she? Most women are desperate to get their daughters married off."

"Most women but not Mother. She's already seen me married and she doesn't seem keen to do it again."

Mr Jackson paused and looked out over the river, which was now in front of them. "I can see you're nervous, but I'll tell you what, why don't you let me walk you home tonight? If she's still downstairs, you can introduce us. I promise I'll be on my best behaviour." A dimple appeared in his left cheek as he grinned.

"I don't know."

"She has to find out sooner or later." Mr Jackson raised an eyebrow.

Ann twisted her fingers together. "Why? Can't this be our secret?"

"Not if you want us to have a future together."

Ann's heart skipped a beat. "You want us to have a future together?"

"I do." He took her hands and kissed the back of each of them. "I hope you don't think me forward, but I wonder ... will you be my wife?"

The blood drained from Ann's face and Mr Jackson caught hold of her as she stumbled backwards.

"Let me find you a seat." He scanned the footpath before escorting her to a nearby bench. "Here, sit down; I didn't mean to shock you."

Ann took several deep breaths. "Forgive me, but, well, I wasn't expecting a marriage proposal."

Mr Jackson kept an arm around her shoulder. "And the fact that you came over all peculiar, is that a good sign or a bad?"

With her senses returning, Ann grinned. "I should hope you know it's good. I'd be delighted to marry you."

"Splendid!" Checking that no one was watching, he kissed the end of her nose. "We'll be so good together."

"Mother might still be a problem though."

"Nonsense. You're your own woman."

Ann grimaced. "I'm not twenty-one until October. We'll need her approval if we want to marry before then."

A frown crossed his face as he stared at her. "That shouldn't matter. You've already been married. The fact your father's already given you away means it's up to you if you want to marry again. Not anyone else."

Ann's eyes narrowed before a smile developed. "You're right. Mother's continued to give the impression that she's my guardian, but she isn't. I can do what I want."

"So, you'll marry me despite your mother?"

Ann squeezed his hands. "I will."

"Well, that's settled then." He took her hands and kissed the back of each one for the second time. "You must call me Chas from now on, no more Mr Jackson."

"Chas. I like that. And you may call me Ann."

"Ann. Ann, Ann, Ann. I love the name already." He laughed as he spoke but suddenly became serious. "You do realise that if we're to be married, I probably should meet your mother."

Ann sighed. "I suppose so, but not now. Can we keep it to ourselves a little longer? I don't want to spoil anything and it's so pleasant sitting here." She studied the myriad of sailing boats on the river before them. "I just want to remember tonight as it is. Mother can wait."

Chas pulled her closer to him. "Very well. This shall be our night, but tomorrow you must let me walk you home. I have to meet her sooner or later; I don't know why you're so reluctant."

Ann rested her head on his shoulder. *Oh, you will.*

CHAPTER EIGHT

Ann was out early again the next morning and as usual Chas was waiting for her. She slowed her step when she saw him. Was it her imagination, or did he look especially handsome this morning? She guessed he had a new shirt on under that rather dashing cravat and had he styled his hair?

He smiled when he saw her. "What are you dawdling for?"

"Nothing." She batted her eyelashes at him. "I was just admiring the view."

"Were you now? I'll have to watch for that." He offered her his arm as they set off down St John Street. "Are you all set for telling your mother?"

Ann grimaced. "I didn't sleep much last night, if that's what you mean."

"Oh my dear, please don't worry yourself."

"It wasn't all worry." She bit on her lip and waited for him to face her. "Part of it was thinking about you."

He chuckled. "So I wasn't the only one having illicit thoughts. Come on, let's get this shopping done and we can get your mother dealt with. We need to be married as soon as possible."

Ann's pace slowed. "Do we have to speak to her? Don't you wish we could just run away together and be married without telling anyone?"

"A clandestine marriage you mean? I'm sure your mother would be more upset about that."

"Maybe, but at least then I'd have you to protect me when she found out. At the moment, she's got used to me being around the house." *Not to mention the money.* "I just don't think she'll be happy."

"Well, I think you're exaggerating. I've borrowed my uncle's top hat again so she won't know I'm a Quaker and we can speak to her as soon as you have your shopping. I won't take no for an answer."

Ann dithered over every purchase until she could delay returning home no longer, but even then, her pace was slow.

"Is that it?" Chas pointed to the small wooden-framed building that appeared squashed between its taller neighbours. "I must confess I didn't pay much attention to the house when I first saw you. I had other things on my mind."

"It is. It might not be big, but at least it's ours."

Chas eyed the property. "It's not to be sniffed at. Your mother was fortunate. Actually, thinking about it, did you ever tell me her name? I presume it isn't Mrs Evans."

Ann giggled. "No, she's Mrs Davies, you'd better not get that wrong."

Ann pushed open the front door and stepped into a small hallway that led to the stairs. She blinked several times to adjust her eyes to the gloom before closing the front door behind them. "Wait here a moment and I'll see where she is …

leave your hat on the table." She tentatively turned the knob on the dark wooden door and peered into the living room to see her mother in the armchair by the window.

"You've finally brought your fancy man to see me, have you?"

Ann's heart skipped a beat as her mother's black eyes bore into her.

"Y-you saw us?"

"I've been waiting for you. Jane told me you've been meeting him for weeks when you were supposed to be listening to the preachers and yet you haven't had the common decency to tell me."

"Jane...?" Ann froze. *I told her in confidence.* She opened her mouth to speak, but Chas distracted her as he stepped into the room.

"Mrs Davies, I believe." He extended a hand, but Mrs Davies stared at him while keeping her knitting clenched firmly on her lap. He hurriedly put his hand behind his back. "Yes, well, I don't suppose we need such formality. I'd like to introduce myself, I'm..."

"I'm aware of who you are, Mr Jackson, and I know what you are." She looked him up and down. "What business do you have with my daughter?"

"We've been walking out together for a couple of months and I've asked her to be my wife. We'd like your approval."

"My approval!" Mrs Davies laid down her knitting and stood up, pulling herself to her full height, which just reached Mr Jackson's shoulder. "You have no such thing. My daughter's barely out of mourning for her late husband and you come here to take advantage of her."

"No, it's not like that..." Ann said.

"You keep out of this." Another glare from her mother sealed Ann's lips. "You've already shown what a dunderhead you are, I'll deal with this."

"Mrs Davies, forgive me for saying, but we've never met before. How can you dismiss me when this is the first time we've met? I know Ann's been through a lot over the last few years and I want to take care of her."

"I think you'll find I'm perfectly capable of doing that myself. She doesn't need a *Quaker* to look after her."

Chas shook his head. "I fail to see what difference that makes."

"Which goes to show your unsuitability. Now, begone with you. I don't want to see you with her again. Do you understand?"

Chas stepped forward, the colour rising in his cheeks, but Ann caught his arm.

"No, please don't say anything. Let me show you out."

He gaped at her, his mouth set in a hard line.

"Please, it's for the best."

With a curt nod he followed Ann to the door and out into the hallway where he picked up his hat.

"Keep walking," Ann said as they stepped outside and headed down St John Street. "I'll tell you when to stop." She led him away from the house to a spot her mother couldn't see from the window. "I'm sorry, but I did warn you." Her cheeks burned as she stared across the street, blinking back her tears.

Chas's voice was brusque. "Are you going to stand by and let her tell you what to do?"

Ann wiped her eyes. "What else can I do? I don't want to fall out with her."

"What about me? Do you want us to stop seeing each other?"

Ann hung her head. "No, of course I don't. I want us to carry on as we were. Can't we just let her think we're not seeing each other any more?"

He lifted her face to meet his gaze. "But we would still see each other?"

Butterflies churned in her stomach. "If you'll still have me. I love you and I'm not going to let her keep me from you. I'll still go to the market every morning and she doesn't know that that's when we meet each other. We can carry on doing that, it's only evenings we'll have to avoid. For now."

Chas's face was stern. "Very well. Let her think she's won, but she's not heard the last of this. I'll get a licence for us to marry ... we can make it quick."

"No, not too quickly."

Chas's brow furrowed. "You said you wanted a clandestine marriage."

"I did, but not yet. My husband's not been dead six months and we've not known each other long. I don't want people talking ... saying we had to get married, if you understand my meaning. If we could just wait another couple of months..."

Chas nodded. "Very well, but not for too long. I won't be told who I can and cannot marry."

Ann sighed. "No, it won't be for long, I promise. Now, I'd better go before she comes looking for me."

Ann knew she needed to hurry home, but as soon as she was visible to her mother, her pace slowed. *What do I say?* She stopped to pick up some litter, but unable to delay the inevitable, she pushed open the front door and went inside.

Mrs Davies stormed from the living room door as Ann stood in the hall. "How many more secrets are you keeping? I brought you up as a God-fearing child and yet you give me nothing but lies and deceit. You need to get to church and ask for forgiveness."

Ann pursed her lips as she took a deep breath. "I didn't lie, I just didn't mention Mr Jackson. There's a difference."

"Less of your lip."

Tears filled her eyes as the two of them went into the living room. "It's true. I knew how you'd react, that's why I didn't tell you." She wiped the back of her hand across her cheeks. "Why is it so wrong for me to want to marry again? You should be pleased."

"Pleased! When you come home with a Quaker?"

"It doesn't matter. He's kind and considerate, that should be more important."

"Until he gets his hands on your money and then you'll have nothing."

Ann stared at her mother. "Is that what you think? That he wants my money? Well, you're wrong. He knows nothing about it, I haven't told him. Not that it would matter. Didn't you notice how well dressed he was? I'm sure he'll have more than enough money of his own to stop him worrying about mine."

"You fool of a girl." Her mother paced the room. "As soon as you get married, any money you have will be his. Do you want to lose everything? You said yourself, you could get your own house one day, you've no need to tie yourself to another man. Why do you think I never remarried?"

Ann hesitated. "I-I don't know. Because you didn't find anyone to love?"

A high-pitched cackle filled the room. "Love!" Mrs Davies shook her head. "Have I taught you nothing? If I marry again, we'll lose this house and I'm not going to risk that. Now you're a wealthy young woman, you need to learn to trust no one. You're too gullible. It won't matter to any man, Mr Jackson or anyone else, how much money they have already. If they can get their hands on yours, it will do them nicely ... and then you'd be trapped looking after his children while he gives you a couple of shillings a week to pay for everything."

Ann sat down and buried her face in a handkerchief. "It's not like that. He loves me, and I love him. And why shouldn't I have children one day? I don't want to grow old on my own."

"You'll have Jane and Susan. There's no reason you can't all stay together."

Jane. She's behind all this. Ann stood up. "I'm not listening to any more of this; I need to go."

Ann staggered out into the back yard where Jane was beating out the bedroom rug with Susan. As soon as she saw her, Jane handed Susan the stick and hurried towards her.

"I'm sorry, I didn't mean to say anything, but she already knew. She forced me to tell her what you'd been doing."

Ann took a step back and studied those in the yard. "How did she know? You must have said something."

"No, I didn't; please believe me. It sounded like she'd been talking to someone. I didn't tell her deliberately." Jane wrung her hands before her. "You know what she's like."

"Who would she have been talking to? It makes no sense." Had she seen any of the neighbours at the market while she'd been with Chas? She was sure she hadn't. "We need to find out what she's been up to. As far as I'm aware, the only person she ever talks to is ... Father Jacobs!" Ann put her hands to her mouth. "Oh my goodness, *that* makes sense. She almost used the same words as him, too."

Jane cocked her head to one side. "What do you mean?"

"Oh, my dear, I can't tell you, but you must understand it's for your own good. If I don't tell you anything, you can't tell her, accidentally or otherwise."

Jane took hold of Ann's hands and squeezed them. "What will you do?"

Ann's face hardened as an image of Father Jacobs flashed through her mind: his greedy hands outstretched. *He's going to want more money when I get my next payment.*

"Ann! What are you thinking?"

She studied her sister. "I need to pay Father Jacobs a visit."

She'd been to the church hundreds of times before, but today her legs struggled to take her up the steps. She had to do this; she couldn't let a priest and her mother ruin her life.

With her heart pounding she pushed open the heavy wooden door and waited for her eyes to adjust to the gloom.

"Is there somebody there?" Father Jacobs walked down the centre aisle and Ann let the door close as she stepped into the church.

"Forgive me for disturbing you, Father, but I wonder if I may speak to you."

"Yes, of course, my dear." He put an arm around her shoulders as he ushered her to a side pew. "Do you have something for me?"

"N-no. No, I don't. That's what I've come to tell you ... or at least part of it."

A scowl replaced the smile on the priest's face. "Go on."

"Well, the thing is, I believe you told Mother you saw me

with ... with a gentleman."

"I may have mentioned it in passing."

Ann bit her lip. "Did you also suggest that I shouldn't be walking out with any gentlemen, lest they ask for my hand in marriage?"

"I'm sure I wouldn't have said any such thing..."

"That's what I thought. It just seemed strange that when Mother mentioned it to me, she used very similar words to the ones you used when you warned me about other men. You both told me I should trust no one. Why would that be?"

Father Jacobs gave a nervous laugh as he patted her hand. "I'm sure it's nothing more than a coincidence. Your mother's a worldly woman, she knows about these things."

"Yes, that must be it. Well, I'm sorry to have taken up your time." Ann stood up to leave but the priest blocked her exit.

"Aren't you forgetting something? The tithe."

"Oh, no." Ann held her hands together to stop them shaking. "Mother wasn't happy about me giving you so much money and so she's taken it from me and hidden it for safekeeping. I won't be able to give you any more."

Father Jacobs pressed his lips together. "I'm sure there's been a misunderstanding, nevertheless, you'll be due another twelve pounds ten shillings shortly. It is rather a lot of money for a young girl like you and you must admit it would be selfish to keep it all to yourself. The church only needs a tenth of it."

Ann prayed that the dim light hid the burning in her cheeks. "I'm sorry, but it's up to Mother now."

The priest's mouth twisted. "Very well, but if I could give you another word of advice; if you're trying to hide something, reinstating the tithe may be in your best interest."

CHAPTER NINE

Leaving Chas on the corner of Compton Street, Ann walked the last hundred yards to the house, alone. The sun was pleasantly warm and she was in no hurry. As usual, Chas watched her until she reached the bend in the road and she waved before disappearing from his view. She pushed open the front door but stopped when she heard voices coming from the living room.

Father Jacobs. What's he doing here? Taking a deep breath, she walked straight in. "Good morning, Father."

"Ah, Mrs Evans." Father Jacobs stood up as she entered. "I haven't seen you for a few weeks."

"No, I've been rather busy. Was it me you came to see, or Mother?"

"Both of you as it happens. Won't you sit down?"

Ann declined the chair he offered and walked to the window. "I suppose Mother's told you about Mr Jackson?"

"Mr Jackson?" The priest turned to Mrs Davies.

"Wash your mouth out, girl, and apologise to Father Jacobs immediately."

Ann's heart pounded in her chest. "What am I apologising for? I thought you'd want him to know we're no longer walking out together. It will save him looking for us. Isn't that why you're here, Father, to make sure I don't find myself another husband?"

"I-I'm sure I d-don't know what you're talking about." The jowl under his chin shook as his head bobbed between Ann and her mother.

"Then surely I'll apologise. In that case, I presume you've called to get your money from me." Her heart beat with such force that she thought it would break from her chest.

Mrs Davies's eyes narrowed as she stared at the priest. "What money would you want from Ann that doesn't go on the church plate?"

"T-The tithe..." The priest's eyes were like pinpricks.

"I've already told you; tithes should be graciously accepted for the good of the poor, not coerced for those who don't need them."

"Yes, naturally ... but Mrs Evans offered..." He twirled his hat in his hands.

"She did no such thing. Neither did she offer to buy you a new hat." Mrs Davies glared at the priest.

"And I came to tell you there'd be no more." Ann's cheeks were burning.

"Well, yes, but as I pointed out, twelve pounds ten shillings is a lot of money for a young girl..."

"May the Lord have mercy on you, Father. As long as my daughter's under my care, you will not take her money."

The priest's cheeks huffed. "It really isn't what you think..."

"Well, in that case we'll say no more about it. Was there anything else?"

The priest shrank back in his seat before he stood up and replaced his hat. "No, not today. If you'll excuse me, I'll let myself out."

He hadn't left the room before Ann collapsed into the nearest chair. Her heart was racing as the perspiration on her forehead stuck her hair to her face. Her mother disappeared into the scullery and came back with a cup of water.

"Why didn't you tell me he wanted more money?"

"I didn't know he did. I went to see him after he'd told you about Mr Jackson to ask why he'd done it..."

"What do you mean?" Mrs Davies's brow furrowed.

Ann held her mother's gaze as she drained the glass of water. "When you met Mr Jackson, you used the same words about trusting nobody that he'd used at the funeral."

"I'm sure it must have been a coincidence."

Ann shook her head. "No, I don't think so. When I asked him why he'd spoken to you, all he was interested in was the tithe. When I said he wasn't having any more money, he said that if I wanted to hide anything from you, I should reinstate it."

Mrs Davies lowered her eyes to the floor.

"That was why I wanted him to know I'm no longer seeing Mr Jackson. So he couldn't threaten me."

Mrs Davies shook her head. "He's made fools of both of us."

"Is that why he doesn't want me to get married, because he thinks a husband would put an end to his supply of money?"

Mrs Davies flicked her eyes to her daughter before reaching for a handkerchief. "I'm sure I've no idea."

The following week as she left the house, Ann closed the front door behind her and smiled at the sun as it bathed the far side of the street. It felt good to be out when the air was warm, and it was even better knowing that Chas was waiting for her while Mother knew nothing of it.

As usual, her stomach fluttered when she saw him on the corner of Compton Street. He was so handsome and had the loveliest smile. There was always that twinkle in his eye, too. Well, almost always. Ann's brow creased. Today was different.

"Is everything all right?"

He pressed his lips together as he offered her his arm. "It is now you're here..."

"But?"

Chas remained silent as they set off on their usual route.

"Please tell me." Ann stopped and stared up at him. "What is it? We shouldn't have secrets."

Chas ran a hand across his face. "I've got something to tell you, but I'd like us to walk for a while first."

Ann's eyes narrowed. "Can't you tell me while we're walking?"

They set off again, Chas keeping his eyes firmly in the distance. "I'm afraid to say, I have to go away."

"Away?" Ann's knees crumpled, and he reached out both arms to support her.

"Oh, my dear. I knew this would happen; that's why I wanted to be by the river before I told you. You need to sit down." He ushered her to the edge of the footpath where she could lean on the wall of a house. "This will have to do."

Ann's eyes were wide. "Where are you going?"

"I had a letter from my mother after I saw you yesterday. She needs me back in Birmingham."

"Tell me it's just for a visit. You will be back?"

"Of course I'll be back." He took hold of her hands. "I just don't know when. It could be weeks."

"Weeks!" Ann's eyes glazed over. "What will I do without you? I live for our mornings together, they're all that get me through the rest of the day."

"I'm sorry ... but Mother's letter sounded urgent. I have to go."

"Didn't she say what she wanted?"

Chas studied the ground as he shook his head. "Something about the family business..."

Ann bit on her lip and took a deep breath. "Could I come with you and...?"

"No!"

Ann banged her head on the wall at the ferocity of his tone.

"I-I'm sorry, I didn't mean to shout. Come here." He pulled her close. "I have to do this on my own. As soon as it's over, I'll be back and we'll be married, no matter what anyone says."

Ann wiped away the tears threatening to erupt from her eyes. "You promise?"

"I promise." He bent down and kissed her gently on the lips. "I love you, why would I stay away any longer than I have to?"

Ann nestled into his chest breathing in the smell of his manliness. "I don't know but I think I shall die if you leave me for too long."

He stroked his hand down her back. "I won't be gone any longer than necessary. I promise."

Ann straightened up to wipe her eyes but froze as a figure dressed in black floated past them.

"Father Jacobs." She indicated towards the older man. "What's he doing here?"

Chas shrugged. "It's a busy road, why shouldn't he be here?"

A chill ran down her spine. "Do you think he saw us?"

"I would say so. Why wouldn't he?"

Ann's voice struggled to escape from her dry mouth. "I think he's watching us."

"Watching us?" The creases on Chas's forehead lifted as his eyes widened. "You think he'll tell your mother?"

Ann nodded. "I do."

"But why would he do that? It makes no sense."

Ann bit down on her lip but could only shake her head. "I've no idea."

Chas studied the back of the priest as he disappeared down the road. "Thinking about it, I'm sure I've seen him at the market over the last few days."

"You've not!" Ann's mouth fell open, but she hurriedly closed it again. *The blackguard.*

"I have. I hope I've not got you into trouble."

Ann spoke with a conviction she didn't feel. "I'm sure I'll be fine, and once you go away, there'll be nothing for him to tell."

Chas turned back to face her. "You're right but if he's on his way to the market, I'd better not go with you. I should leave now." He bent to kiss her forehead. "I'm sorry, but it's for the best. This way you can deny ever seeing me. Besides, I have a carriage picking me up at noon..."

"Noon?"

"I couldn't give you any more warning, I didn't have much myself. I'll write to you..."

Before she could answer, he kissed her again and hurried away, leaving her alone. She remained where she was, staring at the corner of Compton Street long after he had disappeared, willing him to return.

She was numb. *He's gone. How could he?* Eventually, the crowds in the street increased to the point where she had no option but to turn and head towards the market. *Confound Father Jacobs. If it hadn't been for him... But what was he doing? Would he really tell Mother? Or would he keep it to himself if I give him the tithe?* She shook her head. *He's a man of God, he wouldn't do that.*

She sighed. *He would do that, but I'll beat him to it and say we met each other by chance. She's no way of knowing it was planned ... and I can tell her Chas has gone. At least that much will be true.*

She trudged around the market stalls paying little attention to the produce on offer. She bought nothing more than three slices of liver and some potatoes. She wasn't hungry. There was no point wasting money.

By the time she got back to the house she was expecting to face the wrath of her mother but was relieved to find it was the maid who was being chastised over dirt on the windows. As if that could be avoided around here.

"Ah, you're back." Mrs Davies followed her as she put the meat in the larder. "Jane was looking for you earlier. Have you seen her?"

"N-no, I've come straight in. Is she in the back?" Ann's forehead creased.

"I expect so. She was with Susan. They perhaps want you to go out with them this afternoon."

"Yes, right." Ann moved to the back door but paused. *Why's she being so nice? Something's not right.* "Before I go, I've something to tell you."

Mrs Davies studied her but said nothing.

"I bumped into Mr Jackson when I was out."

"Oh yes." Mrs Davies folded her arms across her chest.

"Yes ... he, erm ... he told me he's going away. He has to go back to Birmingham."

Mrs Davies relaxed and turned to go back into the living room. "Well, let's hope he stays there."

Ann took a deep breath before following her. "I wanted to tell you before Father Jacobs did. He saw us together ... I expect he'll want some money in return for not mentioning it to you."

Mrs Davies turned back. "Really? That explains a lot. He called earlier and invited me to the rectory for tea."

Ann peered at her mother. "Would he tell you without mentioning it to me?"

Mrs Davies raised an eyebrow. "Maybe he wants to send you a warning."

"Well, at least some good's come out of Mr Jackson leaving." Ann's eyes filled with tears. "I hope you take great delight in telling him he's gone and that he won't be getting any more money from me."

CHAPTER TEN

Ann rolled over and pulled the bedcovers over her head to block out the daylight as it poked around the edge of the drapes. Was it really only a week since Chas had left? Already it was getting harder to climb out of bed despite the sun rising so early. Her stomach churned. She had to get up. Mother had already commented on her sluggishness and she couldn't afford to let her guard down. Chas would be back soon and getting out of bed early would once again prove easy. She couldn't jeopardise their special time for the sake of a few weeks.

She threw back the cover and eased herself off the bed. At least it was warm. After dressing quickly, she was ready to leave the house when her mother sauntered down the stairs.

"Oh good, I've caught you." She handed her a shilling. "I need you to get a breast of lamb for dinner tonight ... and make sure the butcher rolls it properly. We have a visitor coming."

"A visitor? Who warrants a breast of lamb on a Tuesday night?"

"Never you mind, but you'll have to get all the vegetables to go with it."

Ann nodded. "I'll see what I can get."

The creases in her forehead didn't disappear until she was way beyond Compton Street. Who could her mother possibly be entertaining? Her mind raced as she crossed Compton Street and waited for a gap in the livestock trundling down St John Street. She was sure it was getting busier. With no chance to cross, she stopped and looked back. Today was the first time in weeks that she hadn't paused hoping to see Chas walking towards her. Was she forgetting him already? She studied the corner where he used to stand. *It won't be long now.*

By the time she arrived at the market, the crowds had already gathered, and she dodged around everyone as she made her way to the butcher's. Since the incident between Chas and Mr Williams she'd found a new one, but when she arrived, her frown deepened. Where was he? The stall was there, but it was empty. She scanned the nearby stalls, hoping for an explanation but when she didn't find one, she approached a neighbouring costermonger.

"Could you tell me why the butcher's is closed?"

The man shrugged. "Just didn't turn up this mornin'. Said he was a bit off colour yesterday and so 'e's probably taken to 'is bed."

"Oh, I'm sorry."

"Your best bet's to go to Mr Williams up at the top. 'E's got the choice cuts of meat if you can afford them."

"Yes, thank you." Ann took a few steps away from the stall before stopping to look around. Where else could she go? Not all the stalls were reputable, but *Chas had told her not to see Mr Williams again.*

A man pushed past her forcing her to the side. "Come on, luv, out the way." She sighed. *Surely visiting him just this once wouldn't be so bad.*

As she approached the stall, she saw Mr Williams with several women crowded around him. He clearly hadn't lost his patter. *He probably hasn't even missed me.* Not wanting to interrupt, she headed for the stall opposite to buy her vegetables.

"Three carrots, a swede, two onions, a large cabbage and...." She stopped when she heard her name being called from behind.

"Mrs Evans? Well, I never."

Ann turned to see Mr Williams walking from the back of his stall leaving several irate customers waiting. His smile was unmistakable.

"I thought I'd lost you."

For a moment, Ann feared he might embrace her. "I'm sorry?"

"I've not seen you for weeks. Eight to be precise. I was beginnin' to worry I'd never see you again."

"Really? I didn't realise it was so long."

Mr Williams's eyes narrowed as he surveyed the crowd. "You haven't brought that gentleman with you?"

Ann's shoulders slumped. "Mr Jackson? No, he's gone back to Birmingham."

Mr Williams's smile broadened. "Well, that's good news. Now, you come over to me when you've finished 'ere and I'll see what I can do for you."

Ann loaded up her basket with vegetables before stepping

across to the butcher's, thankful there was still a crowd around the stall.

"Come and stand here by me." Mr Williams hurried over and ushered her to the side of the stall that he usually kept free. "Give me a minute and I'll be with you. I've a nice piece of pork if you'd like it."

Ann's cheeks burned as the rest of the customers stared at her. "No, thank you. I need a breast of lamb if you have one."

Mr Williams sucked air through his teeth. "I wish I'd known, I've just let the last piece go. Can I get you one for tomorrow?"

Ann sighed. "Unfortunately not. Mother needs it for tonight." She made to leave. "I'll try one of the other stalls. Good day to you."

"No, don't go." Mr Williams gave up any pretence in being interested in his other customers. "There're all types of charlatans around here, I'll come with you. You need to know what you're lookin' for."

"I'm sure I can manage, Mr Williams. You have customers to deal with."

A row of women nodded their heads as she tried once again to leave.

"Please, I'll be five minutes. Let me see to those waitin' and then I'll put the closed sign up for ten minutes."

"Will the meat be safe with you not here?"

"Now don't you go worryin' about that, it'll all be fine. Just give me five minutes."

Ann had never seen Mr Williams work so fast. He was always so deliberate when he served her. Why couldn't he just let her choose her own meat?

"I'm closing in a minute..." Mr Williams pointed to a new

customer at the back of the queue. "You'll have to wait 'til I get back.

Ann sighed as several women walked away. "Mr Williams, you really don't need to do this."

Without a word, he wrapped a couple of lamb hearts in newspaper and handed them to the waiting customer.

"That'll be tuppence. Have you got the right money? I've no time to give you any change."

Ann wanted nothing more than to slope off, but a minute later, after a quick word with the neighbouring stallholder, Mr Williams pulled out a piece of wood with some writing on it.

"I'll be back in ten minutes." The few women still around tutted as he left. "Now, you come with me, Mrs Evans." He ushered her away from the stall. "Why is it always busy when you want a few minutes to yourself?"

"Perhaps because you're always busy," Ann said. "You really didn't have to do this."

"Now then, Mrs Evans, I'll have none of that. I've a friend just across here who usually keeps a few choice cuts for special customers. The trouble is, he won't serve anyone without an introduction and I couldn't say anything in front of everyone else, but, well ... you're special."

"Why, thank you."

Mr Williams's speech suddenly faltered. "I hope you don't mind me sayin', but ... I've missed you coming to the stall. I thought you'd taken up with that other gent and ... well, it's lovely to see you again."

Ann bit down on her lip as her cheeks coloured. "I'm sure I'm flattered..."

"You will come back tomorrow, won't you?" His face twisted in anticipation. "I'd like that."

Ann shuddered. "I need to get today's meat first."

"Oh, yes, it's just over here." He pursed his lips and ushered Ann towards a stall at the outer edge of the market away from the crowds. "Wait here a minute and I'll see what he's got."

"Oh, I forgot to say, I need it rolled."

"Rolled?" Mr Williams hesitated. "Righto."

Ann pulled her shawl tightly around her shoulders as Mr Williams disappeared behind a sheet of tarpaulin. *What am I doing here?* She surveyed the surrounding area; there were no customers, not regular women like her at any rate. Not for the first time her legs quivered. *I'll give him a minute but no more.*

"Can I help you, luv?" A man came up behind her, a toothless grin on his face. "Don't often see your type around here."

She stepped back as he moved closer. "I'm waiting for someone, but they've been delayed. I'll come back."

She stepped backwards, glancing over the man's shoulders. "If you see Mr Williams, can you tell him I had to go?"

She turned to run but slipped on the mud.

"Careful there, lady." The stranger reached out his hand just as Mr Williams came back.

"What's going on?"

Ann's heart was pounding as Mr Williams stared at her. "Nothing. I nearly fell, but I'm fine. I'm sorry I really must go."

Mr Williams charged at the stranger. "Be off with you. You shouldn't be around here frightenin' young ladies. Go."

He pulled back his right arm but before his fist could connect with the stranger's face, the man had scurried away.

"W-who was that?"

"One of the scavengers, looking for scraps … I'll give him scraps if I see him again." Mr Williams's face softened as he studied Ann. "I'm sorry, I shouldn't have left you for so long, but it was the rolling…"

Ann nodded. "Can you take me back to the main road now? I really need to go."

"Not without this." Mr Williams placed the meat in her basket. "It's the best I could find."

She reached for her purse, but Mr Williams held up his hand. "Please, allow me. I shouldn't have brought you here. You can have it on me."

"I'm sure there's no need for that." She opened her purse but stopped when the smile disappeared from Mr Williams's face. "But it's very kind of you, thank you."

"You will come back tomorrow, won't you?"

Do I have a choice? She allowed the edges of her lips to curl upwards. "If you can get me out of here in one piece, then I'll see you tomorrow."

His relief was obvious. "I'll save a bit of everything for you tomorrow so you can have your pick. God bless you, Mrs Evans."

With dinner time fast approaching, Ann helped Jane set the table for five.

"Has she told you who's visiting?" Ann asked.

"No, not a word. She just said wait and see."

"Yes, she said the same to me. Well, whoever it is, they'd better hurry up. We'll be sitting down in five minutes."

Mrs Davies bustled into the room. "Stop worrying, he'll be here in a moment."

"He!" Ann and Jane spoke in unison causing Mrs Davies to stop.

"All right, if you must know, it's Father Jacobs."

"Father Jacobs?" Ann stared at her mother. "Why's he coming? Does he want..." she paused as Jane hovered around the table "...something?"

Mrs Davies tutted. "Not at all. His housekeeper's been ill for the last couple of days and he can't cook for himself. I thought it was a neighbourly gesture. It can't be pleasant being on your own every night."

"I hope he won't preach a sermon at us," Jane said.

"Enough of that, I want you all on your best behaviour. I don't want him thinking I can't bring up well-mannered daughters."

"He already knows us..."

Mrs Davies cut Jane off in mid-sentence. "Maybe he does, but that's no reason not to be courteous. Now, it wouldn't surprise me if he'd like you to tell him about the Methodist preachers you listen to. He seems very interested."

Ann smoothed her hand over the tablecloth one last time before straightening up. "I'm sure he is."

As she spoke there was a knock on the door and Mrs Davies hurried to open it.

"Father Jacobs, do come in."

Susan took hold of Ann's hand as the priest was shown in.

"Good evening, ladies, thank you for letting me join you this evening." He breathed in. "My, something smells good."

"Oh, it's nothing special, Father. Just some braised lamb."

Ann rolled her eyes. *Don't have him thinking we eat like this every night; he'll definitely want some money.*

"Now, why don't you sit here." Mrs Davies pulled out a chair at the head of the rectangular table. "It may be a bit of a squeeze, but I'm sure we'll manage. Ann, can you get the meat, please?"

The meat had been simmering with a selection of vegetables since midday and it flaked into pieces as Ann carved it onto a serving plate. She put it down in front of her mother as she seated herself to the right of the priest. "Will you serve?"

Mrs Davies simpered at the priest. "I hope you're hungry, Father, because there's rather a lot here." She piled his plate with potatoes and carrots before putting a generous helping of meat on the top.

Ann couldn't help noticing that she got considerably less, as did her sisters, before Mrs Davies helped herself to the surprising amount that was left.

"Now, Father, will you say grace for us?"

With the formalities over, Ann picked up her knife and fork and searched out the few pieces of lamb that nestled between her vegetables.

"Ann, why don't you tell Father Jacobs about the Methodist preachers? I'm sure he'd like to hear about them from you."

Ann put down her cutlery and fixed a smile on her face. "I'm really not sure what to say. What would you like to know?"

The dinner had seemed interminable and the following morning Ann was keen to be out of the house before her mother was out of bed. She was sure she was only asking her so many questions to find out if she really listened to the sermons. Well, she would do from now on.

She reached the market early praying that Mr Williams

would be busy with the early- morning customers, but the stall was quiet, and his face lit up when he saw her.

"Mrs Evans, you're here."

She gave him a polite nod. "I said I would be ... and I wanted to thank you for the lamb. Mother said it was delicious."

His smile dropped. "You didn't have any?"

"Oh, yes, but it was Mother who ordered it..."

"But you enjoyed it?"

"Yes, it was very nice."

Relief spread across his face. "So, what can I do for you today?"

"A piece of bacon, please."

Mr Williams walked to the front of the stall. "You've come to the right place. Here we are, how's this?" He held up the meat but didn't take his eyes off her.

"Yes, that will be lovely, thank you." Ann watched as he took it back to the other side of the counter to wrap. Why was he so much slower than yesterday? She glanced around. *Ah, no other customers.*

The meat was tied into a neat parcel before he walked back and placed it in her basket. "There you go. It should cook up a treat."

"I'm sure it will." She opened her purse. "How much is that?"

Mr Williams ran a finger around his collar. "Mrs Evans, while we're on our own, I wonder ... and I hope you don't think I'm being forward ... but would you allow me to take a walk with you on Sunday afternoon, perhaps down by the river?"

Ann hesitated.

"It would mean the world to me, and now you're on your own..." His face twisted as he waited for her answer.

"I ... I'm sorry, Mr Williams. I'm not on my own." Her heart was pounding. "Mr Jackson's coming back."

Mr Williams's face turned puce. "You said he'd gone away."

"And he has, but I'm expecting him back. Any day now as it happens." She handed him a thruppenny bit. "Please, keep the change."

She couldn't get to the main road quickly enough and her heart was still racing as she waited for a chance to cross. How had she not realised Mr Williams liked her? She shook her head. She hadn't meant to mislead him. Chas would be back any day now; it was already four weeks since he'd gone, which was longer than she'd been expecting. The only thing that mattered at the moment was that she was waiting for him when he arrived.

CHAPTER ELEVEN

Ann lay in bed staring at the ceiling. Was it finally time to acknowledge what she'd suspected for weeks? Chas wasn't coming back. She'd fooled herself into getting up early for three months now so she'd have her alibi when she saw him again. But now she had to admit she'd wasted her time.

She could hear her mother clanking the pots and pans downstairs, but what was the point in getting out of bed? Suddenly the noise stopped and at the sound of footsteps on the stairs, she rolled onto her side and pulled the blanket over her head. She didn't care what time it was; she wasn't getting up.

"What are you doing still in there?" Her mother's voice was sharp as she came into the bedroom. "The butcher won't save the meat until you get there, now get a move on." She pulled the blanket from the bottom upwards before striding over to the window to pull back the drapes. "I want you downstairs in five minutes."

Ann stayed where she was until her mother's footsteps reached the stairs and then pulled the blanket back over her head to hide her tears. The image of Chas that had been so vivid, had become vague. Would he ever hold her again?

The sound of someone running up the stairs jolted her from her thoughts.

"Ann, come on, you must get up. Please." Jane stood breathless at the side of the bed forcing Ann to roll over and look at her.

"What's the matter?"

"Mother's so cross with you she's gone to ask Father Jacobs to come and talk to you."

Ann bolted upright and wiped her eyes. "She's got Father Jacobs coming? She only went downstairs five minutes ago."

"She's just gone to get him and so if you don't want to see him you'd better get up and go ... now. If you're quick, you can be out before they get back."

Ann sprang from the bed and embraced her sister. "What would I do without you?" She pulled her dress over her petticoats and hurried into the yard. At the very least she needed to wash her face. A minute later, she scurried down the ginnel before stopping on the edge of the footpath to check her mother was nowhere to be seen. Once satisfied she wouldn't be caught, she stepped out and headed for the market, keeping her pace brisk until she was out of sight of the house.

She reached Compton Street without pausing for breath. *Keep going, you're not stopping. Don't even look. He's not coming back.* With her head held high she quickened her step until she came to the turning for the market. The road down to the live meat market at Smithfields was blocked with sheep and cattle waiting to be squeezed into pens. Thank the Lord she didn't have to go down there.

As usual, this late in the morning, the stalls at Clerkenwell Green were busy. She slowed her pace while she surveyed the crowds. Her new butcher was unusually busy. Should she swallow her pride and go back to Mr Williams? She hadn't seen him since he'd asked her to walk out with him, nearly two months ago. Her stomach churned. Would he still want to take that walk? It would serve Chas right if he did.

With her head held high, she set off towards Mr Williams's stall but stopped before it came into view. What if he was angry with her? What if he told her he never wanted to see her again? She couldn't bear the thought of being rejected again. No, she'd just have to be patient and wait at her usual stall. She trudged back and waited her turn. The queue moved slowly and by the time she reached the front there was little left. Not that she cared, she wasn't likely to eat much anyway.

"I'll take four slices of corned beef, please." She was rummaging in her purse for the right money when a familiar voice made her freeze.

"Mrs Evans?"

She lifted her face to see Mr Williams staring down at her. There was no smile.

"Did you marry 'im?"

Ann fingered the wedding ring she still wore. She could lie, but what would be the point? She opened and closed her mouth several times before shaking her head. "No. No, I didn't."

"That'll be tuppence, please." The original butcher held out her meat, but Mr Williams took it from him.

"I'll see to this."

Ann fumbled with her change. "Thank you. It's nice to

see you again, Mr Williams, not that I expected you to be here."

"I work here now." He nodded to the man beside him. "We've gone into partnership; it makes it easier ... especially if I ever need to leave the stall."

"Yes, I'm sure it does. Well, I'll let you get on, good day to you."

She turned to leave but Mr Williams shouted after her. "Didn't he come back?"

She closed her eyes and took a deep breath as she shook her head.

"So there might still be a chance for us?" His voice was softer now and closer as he came up behind her.

"I don't know that there was ever a chance."

"But you'll take that walk with me?"

Ann stared down at the ground, her heart pounding as he walked round to face her. "Very well."

The familiar smile returned to Mr Williams's lips. "Splendid. Shall we say Sunday? I can call and collect you."

Ann shook her head a little too vigorously. "Oh no, please don't go to any trouble. I can meet you here, in the square. I can be here for two o'clock."

Sunday arrived before she was ready, but as soon as her dinner plate was empty, Ann stood up and cleared the table.

"We'd better hurry if we're going to listen to the preacher."

"There seems to be one a week at the moment." Mrs Davies moved from the table to an armchair by the window.

"They're very popular, that's why. Susan, will you fetch the shawls while I wash these? I'll have my blue one." Ann watched as her young sister hurried up the stairs.

"You're in a hurry this afternoon."

"Yes, I've heard this pastor is very good and so we want to get a good place to stand. Are you ready, Jane?"

"I am; I'll get some water and give you a hand with these."

Mrs Davies followed them into the scullery. "I must come with you to see what all the fuss is about."

Ann's heart skipped a beat. "*Today*?"

"No, not today; I've arrangements for this afternoon, but one day I might surprise you."

"I'm not sure you'll like it. There are no seats."

"Nor hymns," Jane added, as she disappeared through the back door.

"Well, a lot of other people seem very excited by them; it was Father Jacobs who asked if we could accompany you. You aroused his curiosity when he came for dinner and as much as he wants to see what he's up against, he doesn't want to go alone."

"He's a grown man, why shouldn't he go on his own?"

"Because he's a clergyman in the Church of England. He wants to make it look as if you suggested it."

Ann pursed her lips as she turned away. "It seems very strange to me. What are you doing this afternoon, anyway?"

"Father Jacobs has invited me over for a cup of tea. His housekeeper has had to stop working and I think he gets lonely..."

Ann raised an eyebrow. "Are you sure? He's been paying you a lot of attention recently given he's got enough parishioners to keep him talking for weeks. I hope he's not trying to take advantage of you."

"Don't be ridiculous. I've said my piece to him on the matter of money and it's behind us now. I'm only doing the same as other members of the congregation and helping him out until he gets a new housekeeper." Mrs Davies turned and walked back to the living room.

Ann grimaced as Jane came through the back door with a bucket of water.

"What's the strange face for?" Jane poured the water into the stone sink.

"Sunday afternoons are the only time we get to ourselves and she's decided she wants to come with us."

"What, today?"

Ann kept her voice low. "No, fortunately not. She wants to bring Father Jacobs with her so he can see what he's up against."

Jane rolled her eyes. "That will be a shock for him."

"I'm not bothered about him; I'm more bothered about me."

Jane giggled. "No more sneaking off, you mean?"

"That's exactly what I mean; do you think she's doing it on purpose?"

Jane shrugged. "She hasn't asked me about you recently and so maybe they really do want to listen to the preacher."

"Well thankfully it won't be today; now, let's get a move on. We need to go before she changes her mind."

They were almost finished when Susan joined them and within minutes the three of them stepped out of the front door.

"So where are you going today?" Jane asked, as Susan ran on ahead.

"Only for a walk by the river."

"Just like old times." Jane grinned at her.

"No, it's nothing like old times, because I won't be with Mr Jackson." The ache in her chest was still there.

"So why are you going?"

Ann sighed. "That's a good question. I suppose it's partly to help me get over Mr Jackson and partly out of guilt."

"Guilt? Why would you feel guilty?"

"It's a long story, but basically Mr Williams invited me for a walk months ago and I wouldn't go because I thought Mr Jackson would be back. He was rather upset and so when he asked again, I couldn't think of a reason to refuse."

"Oh, to be so popular." Jane feigned a swoon. "Do you like this Mr Williams?"

Ann shrugged. "He's a good butcher and always has a cheery smile for me. As for anything else ... shall we just say he isn't like Mr Jackson?"

"But he has the obvious benefit that he's in London and Mr Jackson isn't. So, do you think you're over Mr Jackson now?"

I don't think I'll ever be over him, confound him. "I hope so."

They reached the junction where Jane and Susan needed to turn off.

"I'll wait for you here when I get back," Ann said. "I can't possibly let Mr Williams walk me home. If Mother sees me with another man, that will be the end of my outings."

"Well, have a nice time, I'll tell you about the sermon."

Ann continued to Clerkenwell Green. It was strangely quiet without the stalls being open. How nice it would be if she could shop in such peace. Mr Williams was already waiting for her in the centre of the square and Ann had to admit he was rather dapper in his Sunday best with his hair brushed back. As usual, he wore a big grin.

"Good afternoon, Mrs Evans. May I say how lovely you look."

She glanced down at her cream dress. "Yes, thank you."

He offered her his arm. "May I?"

She hesitated for a moment, but seeing the swell of his chest she slipped her arm into his and allowed him to lead the way.

"I hope I haven't stopped you doing anything else this afternoon," he said.

"If I wasn't here, I'd have gone to listen to the Methodist preacher outside St John's, but they come around regularly and so I'm sure I can listen again."

"I've never done that, myself." His face hardened. "I prefer to go to church of a Sunday morning and take some time to myself in the afternoon. I like to watch the boats on the river if the weather's nice."

"Really? I would never have guessed. You're quite different when you're not in your working clothes."

"I should hope so. It wouldn't do me any good to take a lady walking with blood on my apron."

"No, I don't suppose it would." Ann saw no hint of a smile on his face. "So, tell me about the business. Why did you go into partnership?"

"It made good sense..."

Ann wasn't interested in the stall, but Mr Williams had become animated and seemed relieved to have something to talk about. He gabbled on as they walked, giving her little chance to join in, but he was pleasant enough and it meant she didn't have to pay much attention. *I suppose this is what normal men are like. Serious and focussed on their work. Maybe Chas is different because he's from Birmingham. Perhaps it's just London men who are like this.* She shook her head. No, Thomas had always had a serious side and never asked her opinion. Thinking about it, she didn't remember ever seeing a playful glint in his eyes.

"Is something the matter?" Mr Williams's brow was furrowed.

"I'm sorry, no, why should there be?"

"You shook your head; did I say something that offended you?"

"Oh that, no, sorry, my ... erm, my hat wasn't sitting right on my head and so I just wanted to adjust it." She shook her head again. "Even the smallest movement can make a difference."

"Ah, I see. Good, now where was I? Oh yes, the butchering."

Jane and Susan were waiting for Ann when she returned.

"You must have got along well if you've been walking all this time," Jane said.

"I'm sorry, I couldn't get away. He's pleasant enough, but he wanted to walk me home, which obviously he couldn't do. It took me all my time to persuade him I'd be fine walking with you."

Jane laughed. "Will you see him again?"

Ann's shoulders sagged. "I don't have much choice. He made me promise I'd be at the meat stall tomorrow and he wants us to walk out again next Sunday."

"You could have said no." Jane raised an eyebrow.

"I could have done, but he was pleasant enough, and looked so nervous I didn't have the heart to turn him down."

"Will you get free meat from him?" Susan peered out from the far side of Jane.

"You weren't supposed to be listening, madam." Ann's cheeks flushed as she grimaced at Jane. "Please don't say anything to Mother, will you?"

"I won't ... but Mother will be happy if you get free meat."

Ann rolled her eyes at Jane. "We're not getting free meat. Even if he offered it, I wouldn't accept. I don't want him thinking that's the only reason I'm walking out with him."

"Or that he can woo you with a nice piece of beef!" Jane giggled.

"All right, that's enough. I'll meet him next week and see how it is. Now, can we change the subject? How was the sermon?"

CHAPTER TWELVE

Peering through the living room window onto the street outside, Ann let out a sigh of relief.

"I think the rain's gone off."

Mrs Davies settled into the armchair beside her. "Even so, I don't suppose that preacher of yours will turn up today. In fact, I don't suppose they'll be around for much longer now that winter's upon us."

"I imagine they will," Jane said. "The Methodists are very popular and they're keen to spread the word of God. I can't imagine a bit of wind and rain will stop them."

"They should never have split from the Church of England," Mrs Davies said. "They still believe in God, don't they? Why have all these divisions?"

"It was the Church who forced them out not the other way around," Ann said. "They're much more enthusiastic and inclusive than the old church and they teach people about the Bible rather than threatening them with it. You should be glad we're interested."

"Well, Father Jacobs isn't happy, that's for sure," Mrs

Davies said. "He's seen his congregation halved in the last couple of years."

"Perhaps he should try harder. If the church was a more agreeable place, maybe more of us would go." Ann turned to Jane. "Are you ready?"

Jane nodded. "I am, but we need to wait for Susan; she'll be here in a minute."

"I might come with you and see what all the fuss is about." Mrs Davies stood up and headed for the door.

"Now?" Ann put a hand to her chest. "I don't think today's the best time to go to your first talk. As you said, he might not turn up ... and it looks like it could rain again. I'd say you'd be better waiting until next week."

Mrs Davies returned to the window. "Perhaps you're right, but I would like full details of what he talks about ... from all of you."

Ann could have sworn her mother stared at her for longer than the other two, but as soon as Susan handed her her shawl, she headed for the front door. "We'll see you later."

"That was close," Jane said once they were clear of the house.

"I know. I'll have to warn Mr Williams that I might not be able to see him next week; he'll have to make do with me calling at the stall."

"So you've already decided he'll ask you again. Is this a permanent thing now?"

Ann shrugged. "Maybe. He's pleasant enough, but we've only been seeing each other for about six weeks ... or is it seven? It's too early to say."

"And he's not asked for your hand in marriage yet?"

"Don't be silly and even if he does, I'll tell him he has to meet Mother first. That will give me a good reason to decline."

Jane chuckled. "Would you really turn him down?"

Ann grimaced. "I'd rather he didn't ask. If I'm to even considering marrying him, I need more time to get to know him."

"Can we meet him?" Susan asked.

"Who, Mr Williams?"

"Yes!" Jane grabbed hold of Ann's arm. "Why didn't I think of that? In fact, why don't you bring him to the meeting. You need to listen to it, so bring him with you."

Ann grimaced. "He wasn't very keen when I mentioned it a few weeks ago."

"Well, if he wants to marry you, he needs to do the things you like." Susan's tone was determined.

Oh if only that were true. "That would be nice, but things don't always work out like that. Besides, who said I'm marrying him? He hasn't even asked me yet."

"But he might ... and it would be better if we could meet him first so we can tell you if we like him," Susan said.

Jane couldn't suppress her grin. "You have to admit, she has a point. I think you should invite him to the meeting and see what he says."

Ann sighed. "All right, but why don't you walk with me to meet him. I'm sure he's more likely to agree to coming if you're with me."

Mr Williams was waiting for her at their usual spot.

"Mrs Evans?" A frown replaced his smile as he eyed Jane and Susan.

"Mr Williams, these are my sisters."

"Delighted, I'm sure." Mr Williams gave a slight bow.

"They've come to ask if you wouldn't mind joining us at the meeting this afternoon."

A muscle in Mr Williams's cheek twitched. "The Methodist meeting?"

"That's the one. Mother was threatening to join us today, but I haven't told her we've been walking out together and so we persuaded her to stay at home. The problem is, to make up for it, she wants us to tell her about the sermon when we get home and so we need to be there."

"Well, that really is most unfortunate." Mr Williams's nostrils flared.

Ann bit her lip. "Perhaps, but it would have been more unfortunate if Mother had come with us. I wouldn't have been able to meet you at all. In fact, I need to warn you that should I miss any of our meetings, it'll be because she's with us."

Jane nodded in agreement. "She wants to learn about the Methodists all of a sudden."

"Given I have little choice–" he offered Ann his arm "– shall we go?"

With further rain threatening, the crowd was small and Jane and Susan stood in a sheltered spot alongside the church wall.

"We'll be right behind you," Ann whispered to Jane. "I'd better talk to Mr Williams. He looks rather sullen."

"Are you all right?" Ann asked when she returned to his side.

He leered at her. "I'm always perfectly fine when I'm with you, but today of all days..." He clenched his fists. "I'd really rather not be here."

"I'm sorry, but as I said, it was either this, or not see you at all. Besides, my sisters wanted to meet you."

"I'm afraid I've not made a very good impression on them. I was rather taken aback." He checked over both his shoulders. "While we're on our own, may I ask you a question?"

"What is it?"

His lips curled upwards, but the smile didn't reach his eyes. "The thing is, I've been thinking about you all week, as I do most weeks if I'm being honest, and well ... we may not have been walking out together for long but it's long enough for me to know that I'd like to spend the rest of my life with you."

Ann put a hand on his arm as her vision swayed.

"The thing is, Mrs Evans, I'd like you to marry me."

"Well..." She lowered her eyes and watched her fingers as they played with a tassel on her shawl.

"Please say you will."

She managed a shallow breath. "It's so sudden..."

"But sometimes you know when these things are right ... don't you?" His eyes were wide as they explored her face. "I do."

Ann shivered and pulled her shawl tighter around her shoulders. "Would you give me time to think about it? I'd also like to speak with Mother. I wouldn't want to do anything she didn't approve of."

"You need to do what's right for you, not anyone else." Mr Williams's face turned a deep shade of red.

Ann stepped over to the wall and put out a hand to stop herself swaying. *Where's that preacher? I wish he'd hurry up.*

A little over an hour later as the preacher left the stage, Ann looked skywards.

"I'd better be getting home. There's a feel of rain in the air and I don't want to get wet."

Mr Williams scowled as he glared at the grey clouds. "A walk would have been nice. Do you mind if I accompany you to Compton Street? We haven't had time to talk today and next Sunday seems such a long time away."

"You'll see me in the week."

Mr Williams harrumphed. "That's hardly ideal, with so many customers. We need to be together for longer."

Ann sighed. "Very well, but we'll be with my sisters."

Mr Williams followed Ann's gaze to Jane and Susan, who were staring in their direction. "I'm sure they wouldn't mind walking a few paces ahead of us."

Ann followed his gaze. "No, I don't suppose they would."

Once the crowd had subsided, Jane and Susan linked arms and led the way home.

"What did you think of the preacher?" Ann asked Mr Williams.

He had a sheepish look on his face. "If I'm being honest, I wasn't paying much attention. I was more interested in you."

"Oh!" Her cheeks flushed. "But surely you must have heard the crowd cheering?"

"I couldn't miss it, although I wondered why they were so excited."

"I told you, listening to the Methodist preachers is different to listening to Father Jacobs. They're much more passionate about the Word of God."

Mr Williams smirked at her. "I can see I'll have to reintroduce you to the church once we're married..."

Ann stiffened. "Would it be a problem if I preferred to find a Methodist church?"

Mr Williams laughed but stopped when he realised she was serious. "We'll talk about it. We can hardly go to separate churches."

"But you could come with me as easily as I could come with you."

He patted her hand. "Come now, let's not have our first argument over which church to go to."

They continued in silence until they saw Jane and Susan waiting on the corner of Compton Street. Ann released her arm from Mr Williams's.

"Shall we say good afternoon here? There's no point going any further."

"If we must." He turned and took her hands. "Please think about the marriage proposal. I promise I'll take good care of you."

Ann studied the ground. "I'm sure you would. Good afternoon, Mr Williams." She tried to pull her hands away, but he kept hold of them.

"Please, call me Amos. We know each other well enough now."

"Very well...Amos." She forced herself to smile. "Now, I really must go." She glanced towards Compton Street to check Jane was still there, but her gaze didn't reach that far before her eyes widened. *It can't be.* Instinctively, she pulled her hands from Mr Williams's, staggering backwards as she did but within seconds, Mr Williams had hold of the top of her arm.

"You said he'd gone away. Is that why you didn't want me walking you home?"

With the sound of her heartbeat ringing in her ears she snatched her arm from Mr Williams and rushed forward. "Chas!"

Chas walked towards them, his eyes like pinpricks. "Is this what you get up to when I'm not here. I told you I'd be back."

"Leave her alone; she's mine now." Mr Williams stepped between them, but Ann leapt to one side.

"Where've you been?" Her voice was shrill. "I did wait, but you told me you'd be gone for two or three weeks ... four months ago! What was I supposed to do? As far as I knew you weren't coming back."

Mr Williams ignored her as he squared up to Chas. "Why don't you go back to where you came from? Mrs Evans and I are to be married in the new year and we don't want you around."

The colour drained from Chas's cheeks as his eyes searched Ann's face. "Didn't you get my letters? I told you I'd write."

Ann's heart pounded as tears threatened to tumble from her eyes.

"I had hoped you'd write back, but you've obviously been too busy."

"And she's going to stay busy; now clear off."

Ann stared at the corner where Jane and Susan stood transfixed. "I'm sorry, I need to go. Mother will be waiting." She lifted the front of her dress and fled, leaving the two men behind her. Jane reached out a hand for her, but she continued running, hoping her sisters would follow her.

She arrived back at the house but couldn't go inside. Not without Jane. She turned around to see her approaching, gasping for breath.

"Are you all right?" Jane leaned on the wall beside her as Susan ran inside.

"Of course I'm not all right." The tears she had held back cascaded down her cheeks. "Of all the times for him to come back ... and I'd waited so long..."

"Is it right that you'll marry Mr Williams? Has he proposed marriage to you?"

"He asked, but I didn't accept." Ann's voice squeaked through her tears. "And how can I even consider it now? Not that Mr Jackson will ever forgive me ... why did he have to see us together?"

"You don't know he won't forgive you."

"Did you see his face?"

Jane shook her head.

"He was so angry. I was frightened he might hit me..."

Jane stroked her sister's back. "From where I was standing, I would say that was the last thing he wanted to do. It was Mr Williams who wanted a fight."

Ann couldn't argue. "But what if he frightens Chas away? I may never see him again."

"If he loves you, he won't just go."

"He won't love me any more; he'll hate me." She swallowed back her sobs. "He'll think I'm a right hussy."

"What's going on out here?" Mrs Davies appeared at the door.

Jane spun round. "Ann's had a shock; she just needs a few minutes."

Mrs Davies's brow furrowed. "While you were listening to the preacher? What sort of people are these Methodists?"

"No, it wasn't the preacher. It ... erm, it was as we walked home."

"What happened?" There was a note of concern in her mother's voice, but Ann couldn't answer.

"She ... well, she bumped into Mr Jackson."

"And he's put her in a state like this?" Darkness crossed Mrs Davies's eyes as she pulled herself to her full height. "Just let me speak to him."

"No!" Ann's voice was fierce. "You've already said enough..."

"I've done nothing but save you from yourself."

"And did you think turning the postman away was helping?"

"Of course it was. I wasn't having you wasting money on letters you couldn't read."

"Wasting money?" Ann's heart pounded. "How many times did you turn him away?"

"Enough to save you at least ten shillings. Now, come inside." Mrs Davies extended her hand to Ann.

"Get off me." Ann pushed past her mother and raced up the stairs before slamming the bedroom door behind her. She never wanted to see the world again.

CHAPTER THIRTEEN

Daylight shone into the room as Ann woke from a fitful sleep, although at what time she'd managed to blank out the image of Chas seeing her with Mr Williams, she couldn't recall. It certainly wasn't during the dark hours of the night when she'd cried into her pillow. She supposed it was exhaustion that had finally made her succumb. She rolled onto her back but quickly cowered under the bedclothes at the sound of heavy footsteps on the stairs. A second later the door opened.

"Are you getting out of that bed today?" Her mother's voice pierced the air. "I opened the drapes in here half an hour ago and look at you. I want some beef shin for dinner, and it'll take most of the day to cook."

Ann put her hands over her face. "I can't go out."

"You can and you will. You should be ashamed of yourself sobbing on the front doorstep like that. Get out there now and put a smile on your face."

With her mother's footsteps fading away down the stairs, Ann forced herself out of bed. How many people had seen her yesterday? Nobody she knew, she hoped. She checked her reflection in the small mirror hanging on the landing wall. Her eyes were red and puffy, but she didn't care.

Without saying a word to her mother, she picked up her shopping basket and left by the front door. Her shoulders slumped at the sight of a large herd of cattle passing by on their way to market. The step would be filthy again by tonight.

Squeezing her eyes together to stop her tears, she bowed her head and turned towards Compton Street. *Compton Street.* Why couldn't there be another way to get to the butcher's? In fact, why did she have to go to the butcher's at all? *Confound Mother.* What was so special about getting beef today of all days? She couldn't face Mr Williams and she needed time to find somewhere else.

Compton Street came into view before she realised, and she stopped abruptly. She couldn't do this. She should have swapped chores with Jane. Anything would be better than this. Without lifting her head, she turned to go back home but froze when she heard her name being called.

Chas? She spun around to see him running across the road towards her.

"You're here; I thought I must have missed you."

Ann stared at her boots.

"Please don't ignore me." His voice was tender as he took her arm and led her down Compton Street away from the noise. "I've been waiting here since daybreak desperate to talk to you. Please tell me it's not true that you'll marry Mr Williams?"

She shook her head as she fumbled for a handkerchief.

"After you left us yesterday, he told me he'd arranged

everything and that you'd said you never wanted to see me again. Is it true? I had to hear it from you."

Ann finally lifted her face to his. "Oh Chas, of course it's not true. I've wanted to see you since the day you left..." She choked back another sob.

"Didn't you get my letters? I wrote to tell you I'd been delayed ... five times. I'd hoped you'd write back."

Without thinking, she leaned forward and buried her head in his chest. "Mother wouldn't accept them."

"Wouldn't accept them? But you knew I'd written?"

Ann shook her head. "No, they must have come when I was out. She didn't mention them because it would have cost too much money."

"She can't do that with someone else's letters." Chas's face was red as he stared at her.

Ann wiped her eyes. "I know, but she knew there was no point accepting them. I wouldn't have been able to read them even if she had paid."

Her body tingled as his arms wrapped around her.

"Oh, my dear, it didn't occur to me. What a numbskull I've been."

"I waited and waited for you ... and then Mr Williams asked me to walk out with him. I thought you'd forgotten about me." Her voice broke again. "I didn't agree to marry him though."

His arms tightened around her as he kissed the top of her head. "Let's at least thank the Lord for that. I would never forget you; you've been in my thoughts and prayers every day."

Ann stayed where she was, wrapped in his arms willing the moment to last forever, but eventually he pulled away.

"I have to ask. Do you want me to leave you alone so you can be with Mr Williams?"

She didn't need to think about it. "No, no, and a thousand times no! I'd agreed to marry *you* and if you'll still have me, then I promise I'll never see Mr Williams again." She wiped her face with her already soggy handkerchief. "Will you forgive me?"

For the first time since he'd returned, his face broke into a smile. "My dear, I'd still want you even if you'd married the cad." He took out his clean handkerchief and Ann laughed as he wiped her face. "How I've missed you."

"I'll warrant it's not as much as I've missed you." Ann's heart fluttered as the glint returned to his eyes.

"Come now, walk to the river with me. We've a lot of catching up to do." He put an arm around her shoulder and escorted her along Compton Street before turning into Goswell Road.

"This is where my uncle lives." He pointed to a house on the opposite side of the street.

"That's very grand. If you can stay there, why were you gone for so long?"

"Mother had got herself into more of a mess than I'd thought. With my sister dying last year, she needed me to help her sort everything out."

"Couldn't your brothers have done it?"

Chas sighed. "They have families of their own and because I worked with Mother before I came down here, it fell to me."

"Can I ask, are your sisters able to read and write?"

Chas nodded. "They can, which is why I didn't give it a thought. I didn't realise how fortunate they were when

Mother insisted they had an education. I assumed it was the same for everyone except the very poor."

Ann shook her head. "Not around here, or in Bristol. Why do we need to read and write when all we'll be doing is looking after a home and family?"

"So you can read letters from people like me?" He raised an eyebrow at her, which she pretended to ignore.

"Is everything sorted out in Birmingham now?"

Chas stared into the distance. "I hope so. I don't want to have to go back again."

Ann squeezed the hand that rested on her shoulder. "That's good. I don't ever want to be without you again."

They walked towards the river past the magnificent sight of St Paul's Cathedral.

"Oh, to be married there." Ann gazed up at the elegant dome.

"I don't think either of us would be considered eligible."

Ann's brow creased. "Where will we be married?"

"In St James's, I suppose, given we both live in the parish."

"But ... you're a dissenter."

He took a deep breath. "There's no law to say I can't be married in a church, it's just the Quaker rules that say I shouldn't be."

"And you're prepared to go against them?" Ann's eyes were wide.

"If that's what I have to do to make you my wife, then yes. I'll speak to Father Jacobs later."

Ann gasped. "No ... you can't. He'll tell Mother."

"Will she still object?"

Ann put a hand to her mouth. "Oh my goodness; she'll be furious with me."

Chas stopped. "Furious?"

"She wanted some beef shin for a stew, but I can't go to Mr Williams after what happened ... and even if I find a butcher who has some left, it will be too late to cook it by the time I get home."

Ann immediately turned towards the market. "Come along, we need to hurry."

Chas hurried after her. "I don't suppose today would be a good time to tell her about the marriage then?"

Ann grimaced. "No, I don't suppose it would be."

Mrs Davies was on the doorstep looking out for Ann when she returned to the house.

"Where on earth have you been? That meat should have been on an hour ago." She took the package from Ann's basket and headed for the scullery.

"I-I had to go to Goswell Road for it, they didn't have any in the market."

"I told you to get out of bed; I don't know what's got into you lately. Now, get up the stairs and get those beds made. Jane's made a start."

"Where've you been?" Jane's eyes were wide as Ann walked into the bedroom and closed the door behind her. "And what happened? Did you speak to Mr Williams?"

Ann shook her head as she helped her sister turn the heavy feather mattress. "Mr Jackson was waiting for me."

"He wasn't! Is that why you're so happy? What did he say?"

Ann couldn't speak quickly enough. "Can you keep a secret? He still wants to marry me."

Jane put a hand to her mouth as she shrieked. "Did you say yes?"

"Of course I did; I never want to be without him again."

Jane threw her arms around her sister. "I'm so happy for you even though I'll miss you terribly."

"I don't suppose I'll be going far, although if I'm being honest, I've no idea where we'll live. We haven't spoken of it. There were so many other things to say."

"What about Mr Williams? Did you see him?"

Ann shuddered. "No. I can't bear the thought of it. He'll hate me."

"Don't you think you'd better tell him you won't marry him?"

Ann sat down on the edge of the bed. "No. I didn't accept his proposal and so as far as I'm concerned, we never were getting married. I think he only said it to upset Chas."

"That's beside the point, he asked you and so I think you should give him an answer. If I came with you would you talk to him?"

Ann squeezed her sister's hand. "That's kind of you but I really can't face him at the moment. Besides, I promised Chas I wouldn't see him again. It's more than I dare given what's happened."

The bedroom door burst open and both girls jumped as Mrs Davies barged in.

"What's going on in here?" She glanced around the room. "These beds should be well finished by now. What are you up to?" Her eyes narrowed as she peered at Ann. "You looked as if you'd been crying all night when you left here this morning and now you have a smile on your face. Tell me what you're up to."

Ann bit down on her lip. *I may not have a better time.* "Mr Jackson's back."

Mrs Davies's back stiffened. "Wasn't he the reason for the tears yesterday?"

"It's not what you think. I was shocked to see him yesterday, but I bumped into him again this morning."

"So that explains why I'll be serving tough meat to Father Jacobs tonight..."

"Father Jacobs. Why's he coming again?"

"Don't change the subject." Mrs Davies stood with her arms folded across her chest. "What are you up to?"

Ann sighed. "I needed to talk to Mr Jackson. I've missed him so much since he went away and seeing him again this morning ... well, it was wonderful." When her mother didn't interrupt, Ann kept talking. "He still wants to marry me."

Mrs Davies sniffed up through her nose. "I've already told you, no daughter of mine will have my blessing to marry a Quaker."

"But does it matter, if we're happy?"

"Does it matter?" The tone of Mrs Davies's voice rose as she spoke. "These people have no respect for the church and make up the rules to suit themselves. They're worse than the Methodists. Well, I won't be party to it. If you marry him, then you're no longer welcome in this house."

Ann's cheeks flushed. "You can't stop us. Father gave me away two years ago and I can make my own decisions."

Ann had never seen her mother's face with so much colour. "If that's your attitude, you can go now."

"You'd throw me out?" Ann glared across the room as Jane lunged forward and skidded to her knees in front of her mother.

"No, please. You can't do that. Didn't you see how upset she was yesterday when she thought Mr Jackson was angry with her? You can't keep them apart forever."

"I can if it means she'll give up the idea of marrying a dissenter."

"No, you can't." Ann faced her mother with her hands on her hips. "I'll never be happy living as a widow knowing that Mr Jackson wants me for his wife. If you want to throw me out, then so be it. I'll go ... and I'll take my money with me." She stormed from the room and dived for the box under her mother's bed.

"Get out of there." Mrs Davies pulled at her feet, but Ann kicked her hands away.

"This money is mine and I'm taking it with me."

"I'll wager that's the only reason he wants to marry you ..."

With the money bag in her hand Ann stood up. "No, it's not. I told you I haven't mentioned it to him and that's still true."

"Well, don't come crying to me when it all goes wrong..."

Ann heard her mother shouting down the stairs after her, but she wasn't listening. She grabbed her cloak and stormed out of the front door, but once it had slammed behind her, she stopped. Where did she go now? Her heart was pounding, and she took several deep breaths before she walked down the steps and headed for Compton Street. *Maybe if God's watching, Chas will be there.*

She reached the corner of the street and gave a deep sigh; he was nowhere to be seen. *What do I do now?* She wandered over to the spot where he so often waited for her. He'd be here again in the morning, but what about tonight? She hesitated, feeling the money bag in the pocket of her skirt. She could pay for a room in a tavern, but people were bound to talk ... and what if Mr Williams heard about it? *What if he does? It's none of his business. But still, he might come looking for me and people would wonder what I'm doing on my own and where the money's come from.* If her mother had taught her one thing, it was not to let people know what you've got.

Her stomach churned as she turned a full circle on the spot. *Dare I go and find Chas?* When they'd walked down Goswell Road that morning, he'd shown her where he was living. Could she just turn up unannounced? She squeezed her eyes shut, determined not to cry. Did she have any choice? She had no idea how to go about getting a room on her own. Thomas had done all that last time. *I need to speak to Chas. He's the only person I trust to tell me what to do.*

CHAPTER FOURTEEN

A nn hesitated as she stared up at the four-storey house. *I'm sure this is the one he pointed to.* She studied the adjoining properties. *Yes, this is it.* She stepped forward and with a deep breath banged on the door knocker. Her heart was pounding, and she was filled with a sudden urge to run, but a maid opened the door before she could turn away.

"Can I help you?"

Ann managed a weak smile. "I wonder if I could speak to Mr Chas Jackson. Is he home?"

The maid looked her up and down before inviting her into the hallway. "Who shall I say is calling?"

With the details she needed, the maid disappeared, leaving Ann in a wide hallway decorated with numerous painted portraits. Many of the men had a similar look across the eyes and she wondered if these were the Jackson ancestors. They looked very prosperous if they were.

"Ann, my dear, what are you doing here?"

Ann wanted to cry as Chas walked down the hall, but she bit on her lip. "I'm sorry, I didn't know where else to go."

He put his hands on her shoulders. "Why do you need to go anywhere?"

"I-I've left home."

Chas's jaw dropped. "Left home? Why?" He pushed open a door. "Come in here and we can talk."

He took her cloak and led her into a reception room at the front of the house that was twice the size of her mother's living room. She wandered over to the remains of a fire and rubbed her hands together. "I told Mother we were getting married."

Chas's face dropped as she recounted the argument. "Oh, my dear, I didn't mean to cause you so much trouble."

"I just don't know what to do..." With Chas's arms around her, her resolve weakened, and she wiped her eyes with the back of a hand. "I've never been on my own before..."

Chas kissed her tears. "And you're not on your own now. I'll speak to my aunt at once and have a room made up for you."

"Stay here?" Ann's eyes were wide. "I couldn't possibly..."

"Of course you can."

"But ... but, it's so grand." She studied the room with its deep red wallpaper and leather chairs.

Chas laughed. "It's not as grand as you think and there are plenty of rooms. Now, do you have a bag with you?"

A bag? She shook her head. "No, I left with nothing. I didn't have time."

"All right, never mind, we'll find some clothes for you. I'm just relieved you came here." He released his hold and gazed at her. "We'll be married as soon as we can be. I'll visit the priest tomorrow."

Ann shook her head. "We can't have any banns read, Mother will try and stop us."

He kissed her forehead. "Stop worrying. You told me once you wanted a clandestine marriage; I'll get us a licence from the bishop and we can be married when we choose. In the meantime, you'll be safe here. Let me get you some tea while I speak to my aunt. Wait here."

A maid had no sooner brought in the tea tray when Chas returned.

"Everything's fine." His presence immediately relaxed her. "She said you can have a room on the top floor and she'll find you some clothes. Once we've had tea, I'll introduce you."

"What about your uncle? Won't he mind?"

"I don't suppose so. He leaves all matters regarding house guests to my aunt, so as long as she's happy you've no need to worry. I'll introduce you to the maids, too." Chas laughed. "Don't look so worried. I'm sure they'll all love you."

Love wasn't the word Ann would have used, but after a full interrogation during which time Chas had been banished to the front room, the large frame of Mrs Jackson led her up two flights of stairs to the attic where she held open a door at one end of a small corridor.

"This is our old nanny's room. It's the biggest of the servants' quarters and so you should be comfortable."

Ann stepped into the room. It had a small window embedded in the sloping ceiling opposite the door and was dominated by a large bedstead that had been covered in an array of blankets.

"It can get cold up here." Mrs Jackson walked to the bed and straightened the top cover. "I'll get a maid to bring up some bed-warmers and light the fire to air the room. Give it a couple of hours and it will be quite snug."

"I'm sure it will be fine, thank you. You're very generous."

"Nonsense, it's the least we could do. We wouldn't want to see you on the streets."

There was a knock on the door and Ann turned to see a young maid she hadn't seen before with a selection of clothes.

"Ah, splendid." Mrs Jackson reached over and took the garments from her. "What do we have here?" She held up a high-waisted white dress, with delicate embroidery around the sleeves and low-cut neckline. "Goodness, I'd forgotten about this. It was my daughter's from a few years ago. The embroidery may be a bit dated now and it may be a little big, but Esther can take it in." She showed it to Ann. "What do you think?"

"I think it's lovely and I'm sure no one will notice if someone like me isn't wearing the height of fashion."

Mrs Jackson beamed at her. "Excellent. We have some gloves to match and a rather nice pelisse here that will go over the top of it, too. It should keep most of the weather off you." She held up a dark grey coat. "Here, try it on."

The pelisse reached down below her knee and Ann pulled it tightly around herself. "I'm sure it's better than the cloak I came in; I was due a new one. Thank you."

"Excellent. Now, I'll leave Esther with you to help you try on the dress, and there are several more, if that one doesn't fit, or you'd like a change. Dinner will be at six o'clock and you're welcome to join us in the drawing room from half past five."

Fifteen minutes later, with the clothes hanging on a couple of hooks in the wall, Esther left to get the bed-warmers and coal for the fire. Ann wandered to the window. She was overlooking the front of the house, but with no cattle in the street, it was strangely quiet. Besides the bed the only other things in the room were a chest of drawers and a wooden chair in the corner under the slope. She pulled the chair to the side of the bed and sat down.

This time yesterday she had been in floods of tears thinking Chas would never want to see her again, and now she was here. She looked around the room once more. A room to herself. What would Jane and Susan say? She was missing them already, but she would visit them as soon as she was married.

Esther knocked on the door and came back in. "Shall I light the fire now?"

"Yes, please. It's a little chilly in here."

Esther knelt down and began stacking the coal.

"Esther, forgive me for asking, but how do I know when it's time to go down for dinner?"

Esther's smile was warm. "Don't worry. There'll be a bell at half past five indicating you can go to the drawing room. As long as you're not late joining them, they'll tell you when to go to the dining room."

Ann bit down on her lip. "Can you tell me ... what do they do in the drawing room? I'm really not sure I should go."

Esther shrugged. "They don't do much. It's usually the time of day Mr Jackson comes home and spends time with Mrs Jackson and any house guests before dinner."

"So they'll expect me to be there?"

"I imagine so. Mr Jackson will probably want to meet you ... but don't worry, he's nice enough. I've had much worse masters." Esther stood up and placed a bed-warmer on the now glowing fire. "There, now would you like me to take that dress in while this heats up? We have half an hour before you need to go down."

With her hair tidied and wearing her new dress and gloves, Ann had never felt more glamourous. She stepped onto the landing while Esther closed the door behind them.

"Don't be nervous, I'm sure Mr Chas will think you look lovely."

She smoothed down her dress. "I hope so, but will you walk down with me? I'm not even sure I can remember where the drawing room is."

Esther chuckled as she went on ahead. "You'll remember soon enough; the house is quite simple really, only three rooms on each floor and the kitchen in the basement."

They reached the bottom of the stairs and Esther led Ann to the back of the house.

"The drawing room door's open; they must have done that for you, it's usually closed."

Ann's heart skipped a beat. *No chance of waiting outside until the last moment then. Please let Chas be here already.*

"Would you like me to introduce you...?" Esther turned around. "Gracious, are you all right, you're as white as a sheet."

Ann took a deep breath. "I'll be fine, if I could just sit down. It's all so formal."

"Take a deep breath. You've nothing to be frightened of."

Ann gulped and a second later followed Esther into the drawing room. Mrs Jackson sat on a long green settee edged with dark wood, which sat opposite the fire. A man she presumed to be Mr Jackson sat in a wing-backed chair alongside her.

Esther gave a slight cough to catch their attention. "Mrs Evans for you, ma'am."

Mrs Jackson twisted in her seat. "Oh, that dress looks splendid. Well done. I knew it would. What do you think, George?"

Mr Jackson peered at her over his newspaper. "Is this the new maid?"

Mrs Jackson rolled her eyes and beckoned Ann to sit beside her. "No, it's not; I told you, it's Chas's young lady."

Mr Jackson put his newspaper down and paid her more attention. "Yes, very nice. Is she here for dinner?"

"Mrs Evans, please forgive my husband, he has a terrible memory for names and details. I was only telling him about you when you walked in. Now, have you made yourself comfortable upstairs?"

Ann perched on the edge of the settee. "Yes, thank you, and Esther's been a great help."

"Well, that's what she's here for. If you need anything just ring for her."

Ann inwardly shook her head. *I've got my own maid!* She perused the room again. The candle-laden chandelier gave out more light that she was used to, but the room was large and it was difficult to see into the corners. Had Chas not arrived yet or was he staying in the shadows to see how she managed on her own? She hoped he wasn't testing her. That would be most unfair on her first night.

"With it being Monday, we're only having a simple dinner of soup followed by a beef stew from yesterday's leftovers. I hope you don't mind. When it's only me and George it seems a shame to waste anything, and Chas is happy to eat it."

Soup *and* stew. "That sounds wonderful." She suddenly

realised she hadn't eaten all day and her stomach rumbled. She pressed her fist into her belly to keep it quiet but stopped when she noticed her dress. White! Oh goodness, there was a reason she always wore grey at home. Perhaps she wasn't hungry after all.

"Sorry I'm late." Ann turned to see Chas stride into the room. "Ann, darling, you're here. I'm sorry, I got rather distracted."

Ann's cheeks burned, and she prayed the light from the chandelier wasn't bright enough to draw attention to it.

"What have you got there?" His uncle pointed to a letter in his hand.

Chas brandished it in the air. "*This* is my distraction. A letter from Mother."

Ann's heart sank. *He can't go away again.*

"What does she want now?" Mr Jackson's smile disappeared.

"She's not asking for anything, she's telling us she's coming to visit."

Mrs Jackson jumped to her feet. "She's coming here? On her own, I hope."

"Not by the sounds of it. It says she'll be bringing several of the girls."

"Several? How many's that! You have seven sisters. I can't find that many beds ... and when's she coming?"

Chas looked back at the letter. "She left Birmingham this morning and so they'll probably arrive on Thursday."

Mrs Jackson put a hand to her head. "Does she never consider asking?"

Ann stood up and edged towards the door. "I'll go. I can find somewhere else to stay."

Chas crossed the room and caught her hand. "You'll do no such thing. We should be putting Mother in a tavern, not you."

"But your sisters..."

Mrs Jackson regained her composure. "The sisters are fine, as long as they don't all come. The spare bedroom on the first floor has two large beds, they'll have to share ... and Ann, would you mind if I put a couple in with you, if necessary? Elizabeth will just have to have one of the smaller servants' rooms. That will teach her not to arrive unannounced."

Chas squeezed Ann's hand as a frown settled on her face. "Elizabeth's my mother."

She nodded. "You'll have to give me a lesson in all of their names. It's as well they won't be arriving for another few days."

CHAPTER FIFTEEN

A nn woke with a start the following morning. Where was she? She glanced around the room and a second later relaxed back into the bed. *Oh yes.* Her heart pounded as the events of the previous day flooded back. Had she really left home? She thought of Jane and Susan. *Jane will have the shopping to do on top of everything. I really didn't mean for that to happen.*

She pushed herself up and looked at the drapes. They were still pulled across the window but it must be morning because a maid had been in to light the fire. She had no idea what time it was. Dare she go downstairs already?

She swung her legs out of bed and moved to the end to sit opposite the fire. She even had a choice of what to wear. She hadn't moved when there was a knock on the door and Esther walked in with a cup of tea.

"Oh good, you're awake."

Ann jumped up. "Gracious, is that for me? I've never had a cup of tea in my room before."

"Mrs Jackson asked me to bring it up for you. Between you and me, I think she wanted to check you were awake."

Ann giggled as she retook her seat. "That's very thoughtful of her. What time is it? I've no idea when I'm up here."

"Almost eight o'clock. The bell will ring at ten o'clock when breakfast is ready. They always take it in the drawing room."

"Ten o'clock. I'm usually in the middle of my chores at that time; we don't eat until midday."

Esther walked to the window and pulled back the drapes. "You're fortunate this morning as well. Mr Chas is joining you. He usually goes out early, but he hasn't today."

Ann covered her mouth with a hand. *I should hope he's not!*

By the time she reached the drawing room, the rest of the family were already gathered.

"I'm sorry I'm late."

Chas jumped up and offered her a chair. "You're not late at all, we've only just arrived ourselves. Now, help yourself to something to eat." He gestured to a selection of breads and cakes. "What would you like to drink? Tea? Or perhaps a hot chocolate."

Ann hesitated. "Can I try a hot chocolate? We don't have it at home."

"Oh my dear, prepare yourself for a treat." Mrs Jackson shimmied in her seat. "I simply can't do anything of a morning before I've had at least two cups. Tell me, did you sleep well?"

"Yes, very well, thank you, and it was nice not having the cattle herding past the window at six o'clock in the morning."

"Yes, I'm sure. They really need to do something about that market. The overcrowding's getting worse by the year."

Ann agreed as Mrs Jackson offered her a selection of cakes. "Thank you, I'll just have the one."

"Is it any wonder she's so thin?" Mrs Jackson offered the plate to Chas. "You'll need to feed her up."

"Nonsense." Chas patted her hand. "She's splendid as she is. Now, my dear, what would you like to do today? You won't have any shopping or cleaning to do. Perhaps you could give me that tour of London you've been promising."

She hadn't promised to do anything of the sort, but why not? "Yes, I'd like that and at least it's dry."

With breakfast over, Ann and Chas left the house and headed towards the City of London.

"I don't know my way around here," Ann said. "I rarely venture out of Clerkenwell."

"Well, we can explore together and for once we needn't rush back."

Ann bit her lip as she formed her next question. "Do you ever go to work, or will we be able to do this every day?"

"I usually call in to see my uncle of an afternoon. He's showing me the ropes of the business so I can start working there when I'm ready."

"You're very fortunate you don't have to work."

Chas cleared his throat. "It's as well I'm not with Mother joining us this week. She really is out of order."

"I didn't think you looked very pleased last night. Is there a problem?"

"Nothing that can't be sorted out, but Mother can be rather overbearing. She's nice enough once you get to know her, but would you mind if we don't immediately tell her we're getting married? I had hoped we'd have done the deed before you met her, but we haven't got time for that now."

"You mean you were going to get married without telling her?"

"Is it any worse than telling your mother and then having to leave home because she objects?"

Ann shuddered. "No, I don't suppose so. Do you think your mother will object?"

Chas spoke slowly. "I'm not sure. I'd like to think she won't but, well ... let's just say I'd rather not upset her as soon as she arrives."

Ann stared at him. "Have you even told her about me?"

Chas said nothing as he continued walking.

"Is this to do with me not being a Quaker?"

Chas stopped and held her face in his hands. "As far as I'm concerned it's of no consequence that you're not a Quaker. I love you just the way you are."

"But your mother?"

He continued walking. "I just need to talk to her..."

Ann pursed her lips together. "Would you let her stop us being married?"

"No, I would not. She might complain, but she can't ... she won't stop us from being together. I'm a grown man for goodness' sake."

Ann clung onto Chas's arm. "What a mess. Why can't the fact that we all believe in the same god be enough?"

Chas spoke through gritted teeth. "Once we're married, that's how it will be."

Ann allowed him to put an arm around her shoulder. "I hope they won't stay too long if we have to wait for them to leave before we can be married."

"I hope so too." He smiled down at her. "I'm sorry I'm being so grumpy, but it would have been so much simpler if she'd stayed in Birmingham."

Ann relaxed. "Have you thought about where we'll live once we're married?"

"We'll stay at my aunt and uncle's, why?"

"Oh. I'd thought we'd get somewhere of our own."

"Why would we do that?" His expression darkened as he fixed his eyes straight ahead.

"Well, to be on our own. When I was with Thomas…"

"No!"

Ann jumped at the ferocity of his voice.

"I don't want to hear about it." He paused and softened his tone. "I'm sorry, but we have no need for a place of our own. We'll be more than comfortable where we are and that's the end of it."

It was mid-afternoon by the time they got back to the house and they joined Mrs Jackson in the drawing room.

"Aren't you receiving any visitors this afternoon?" Chas asked as he ushered Ann to the settee.

His aunt ran the back of her hand across her forehead. "I've had to cancel. With your mother coming, I've too many other things on my mind. At least there won't be eight of them arriving on the doorstep."

"Have you had another letter?" Chas raised an eyebrow.

"Just. She apologises for the short notice but said she couldn't possibly stay in Birmingham any longer with things the way they are."

Chas mumbled something Ann couldn't hear before his aunt continued.

"Anyway, she's only got three of your sisters with her. Eve, Lucy and Rebecca."

"I imagine she's brought Eve to chaperone the other two." He looked over to Ann. "Lucy's about seventeen and Rebecca's a year younger. They've developed a taste for going out on their own. Eve's the eldest and I expect she'll be responsible for them. Mother won't want to do it; she doesn't have a very good impression of London."

"And I can't say I blame her," Mrs Jackson said. "Although I don't think Eve should be left in charge either. When did she last come to London?"

Chas shrugged. "I don't know that she ever has been."

"Well, quite. Given the current situation, I would suggest you chaperone them, and Mrs Evans should accompany you."

The light was still dim the following morning when Ann woke up. The fire had been lit, but the room was still cold; it must be early. She climbed out of bed and wandered to the window. There wasn't much activity.

If she went out now, she'd be back well in time for breakfast and nobody would miss her. She hesitated as she studied the garments hanging on the wall. Overnight she'd decided she had to see Jane and if she was doing the shopping, now would be the time to speak to her.

She selected her old dress and slipped out of the house with no one seeing her. She sped to Compton Street before making her way to St John Street. Should she wait on the corner or go to Clerkenwell Green and hope to find her? A knot formed in her stomach. What if she saw Mr Williams at the market? *I'm not ready for that.* After a moment's deliberation she positioned herself in the spot Chas always stood. It was early enough that Jane was unlikely to have passed yet.

The early morning traders hurried about their business as she waited and even though she'd only been away for a couple of days, the smell and the noise of the livestock was louder than she remembered it. Gradually it grew busier until finally Jane appeared. She had her winter cloak wrapped tightly around her shoulders as she scurried across Compton Street. Grateful she was alone, Ann waved to her.

"Jane, over here."

Jane saw her and immediately hurried over. "Where've you been? We've been worried sick about you." There were tears in Jane's eyes as she hugged her sister.

"Don't worry about me, Chas's aunt and uncle have given me a room. It's you I'm bothered about, having to do the extra chores and all."

"I've managed. Mother has actually been surprisingly nice since you left."

"I imagine she doesn't have a good word to say about me though."

Jane squeezed her sister's hand. "Oh Ann, of course she does. She wants you to come home. We all do."

"Come home?" Ann shook her head. "If that means telling Chas we can't be married then I'd sooner die."

Jane grimaced. "She may listen to reason. Do you want me to ask her?"

Ann hesitated. She was living a different life now. Not only could she spend most of her days with Chas, she had no chores and her own maid. Did she want to go back to being browbeaten by her mother?

"I'm afraid there's no point. I miss you terribly, but even if she lets me come back, it won't be for long. Once I'm married, I'll leave again."

Jane's face dropped. "Well, will you at least come and visit? I can't bear not having you around."

Ann grimaced. "As long as Mother agrees to it and knows I won't change my mind about being married."

A smile flashed across Jane's face. "I'll speak to her as soon as I get home. Will you walk with me so you can tell me all about your new house?"

She linked Jane's arm. "As long as we don't go near Mr Williams's butcher's. I can't bring myself to speak to him at the moment."

They set off down St John Street, joining the growing crowd as they headed in the same direction.

"I saw him yesterday."

"Who, Mr Williams?" Ann slowed her pace. "Did you go into the stall?"

"No, but I walked past, and he saw me. He came running after me and asked where you were."

Ann's stomach churned. "What did you tell him?"

"I told him the truth. I said that I didn't know where you were."

"Did you mention that I'd left home?"

Jane nodded. "He wasn't very pleased. I thought he would hit something, but with only passing shoppers available, he thought better of it."

Ann stopped. "I can't go any further. What if he sees me ... or worse follows me? I'd never forgive myself if he did anything to Chas."

"I'm sure he won't." Jane's face grew serious. "You mean it, don't you?"

Ann glanced around. "He's a nice man, but I've seen him angry with someone before and it wasn't nice."

"I'm sure it wasn't." Jane shuddered. "When will I see you again?"

"I'll be at the same spot tomorrow. Watch out for me ... but please, don't tell anyone where I am. I'm sure there are plenty who'd give Chas's address away for the price of a pint of ale."

Jane gave her sister a final hug. "Don't worry, I won't. I'll see you tomorrow."

Ann hurried back to Goswell Road, checking over her shoulder at every turn to make sure no one was following her. When she finally reached the house, she dashed towards the front door, throwing herself against it, but it stood firm. A wave of nausea passed over her as she rattled the door knob. Someone had locked it. Stepping back to check she had the right house, she bit down on her lip. She'd have to knock. Her hand trembled as she reached for the knocker, but she hadn't let go of it when the door burst open.

Ann stared at Chas as his face changed from relief to anger.

"Where on earth have you been? We've had the whole household searching for you. Have you any idea how much time they've wasted?"

Ann's cheeks were scarlet as tears formed in her eyes. "I-I'm sorry; I didn't think you'd miss me."

He pulled her into the house, slamming the door behind her. "Of course we missed you. Esther took a cup of tea up to your room at eight o'clock and you'd gone."

"I'm not used to being waited on and it didn't cross my mind."

"Where've you been?"

"I needed to see Jane. I've been concerned about her and Susan."

"Here you are!" Esther ran down the stairs towards her. "We were so worried. I'll tell Mrs Jackson at once."

Chas watched the maid disappear. "Have you been near that market?"

Ann wiped her eyes on a handkerchief. "No, I promise I haven't. I turned back before we got there."

"So you planned on going?"

"No, it wasn't like that. Jane wanted to talk and ... I'm sorry."

She turned her face to the floor but relaxed as Chas wrapped his arms around her.

"Don't ever do that to me again, do you hear?" He kissed the top of her head. "I've been worried sick about you."

She relaxed into his embrace but suddenly pulled away. "I said I'd go again tomorrow."

A cloud passed over Chas's face. "Why?"

"Jane said Mother's missing me and wants me to visit; she's going to talk to her and tell me what she says tomorrow."

Chas pressed his lips together.

"Please don't be angry; it's not what you think. I said I'd only visit if Mother accepted that we'll be married."

Chas remained silent for a full minute before replying. "Very well, we'll go together. I don't want there to be any chance of you meeting Mr Williams while you're on your own."

CHAPTER SIXTEEN

The sun was bright the following morning when Ann woke. She stretched out with a smile on her face. How nice it was to lie in bed waiting for a cup of tea ... even though she was going out. Her smile faded as she thought of Jane. She'd mentioned that Mother had dismissed the maid again and so she'd probably cleaned out the fireplaces by now. Ann sighed and swung her legs out of the bed. Perhaps she should go home. A knock on the door brought her back to her senses.

"Good morning." Esther breezed in carrying a cup of tea. "Are you ready for the big day?"

"Big day?" Ann's forehead creased. "I'm only going to see my sister."

"No, not that, Mr Chas's family should be here later. Have you forgotten?"

Ann's stomach somersaulted. "Goodness, is it today? I've had so much else on my mind I've not had a chance to think about it."

"From what I've heard, Mrs Jackson thinks they'll arrive around mid-afternoon. You'll be back by then, won't you?"

Ann took a sip of her tea. "I would hope so unless Mr Chas takes me for a walk. I should be back in time for breakfast after I've seen my sister."

"Oh well, that's something. I'll let Cook know."

Ann watched as Esther tidied around the room. "Have you met Mr Chas's mother before?"

"Not really. I was working here last time she visited, but I was a kitchen maid at the time and didn't see her 'close up' if you get my meaning."

"Did you see her at all?"

Esther chuckled. "It was hard not to. She's quite a large lady and not in the least bit timid. She does her fair share of bossing people around, which is why I think Mrs Jackson always frets when she's here."

Ann's mouth twisted.

"I'm sure you'll be fine, and she should be grateful now you've agreed to give up your bedroom for her."

"I hope she is." Ann may only have been here for a few days, but already she treated this room as her home. "Have you heard how long they're staying? I've grown rather fond of having a room to myself."

"No, I've not heard anything. Besides—" Esther gave her a sly wink "—you'd better not get too used to being on your own with you about to be a married woman."

"Esther!" Ann's cheeks flushed, but Esther laughed.

"I'm just saying. Now, come along. Get this tea drunk and I'll help you with your dress before I move your things downstairs. I'll need to clean the room before they arrive."

Ann hurried down the stairs and breathed a sigh of relief when she saw Chas waiting for her.

"Oh good, you're here. I was afraid Esther might have kept me talking for too long. We need to go."

"Good morning to you as well, my dear." Chas gave a mock bow, causing Ann's cheeks to flush.

"I'm sorry, good morning." She allowed him to kiss her hand. "I've been awake for so long I'd forgotten it was still morning."

"Well, if you've been awake for that long, we'd better go. Your sister is likely to be waiting."

Ann fastened her bonnet before letting Chas hold out her new pelisse while she slipped her arms in. The weather had become noticeably colder over the last few days and she pulled it tightly around herself as he opened the front door and ushered her outside.

"Where are we meeting her?"

"On our corner. It seemed as good a place as any."

They walked quickly and found Jane waiting for them. Ann hurried ahead of Chas.

"Jane, my dear, I'm so sorry we're late."

Jane remained silent as Chas joined them.

"My, I've just remembered, you two haven't met before, have you?" After a brief introduction, Ann turned to her sister. "Did you speak to Mother? What did she say?"

Jane's eyes glistened as she paused. "She's missing you, that's for sure, but ... she wasn't as keen to see you as I thought she would be. She said she wants you to come home and you'll always be welcome but–" her eyes flicked to Chas "–you have to stop seeing Mr Jackson."

Ann stared at Jane in disbelief. "Did you tell her I wouldn't do that?"

"I did, but, oh I don't know. She's just so pig-headed

sometimes. It's as if letting you back while you're still seeing Mr Jackson will undermine her authority."

"She has no authority over Ann." Chas put an arm around Ann's shoulders. "She's a widow, she can do what she wishes."

Ann pulled Jane to her. "Don't cry. I can still see you and Susan. Perhaps on Sunday like we used to."

Jane wiped her eyes. "I'd like that. Shall I meet you here at about two o'clock?"

Ann turned to Chas, who nodded. "I'll come with you. Perhaps we can bring Lucy and Rebecca, too."

Mr and Mrs Jackson were already in the drawing room when they arrived back at the house.

"Oh good, you're here." Mrs Jackson gestured to a maid to bring some hot chocolate. "I wanted to check what you're going to tell Elizabeth about Mrs Evans. Have you told her you plan to marry?"

"No ... not yet." Chas hesitated. "I'm not even sure I'm going to tell her."

"You think she'll object?" Mr Jackson helped himself to a spiced bun.

"I don't know how she'll react if I'm being honest. I had hoped for us to be married first and then I'd tell her later."

"Well, if we're not to tell her, how do we explain Mrs Evans' presence?" Mrs Jackson waved a fan in front of her face.

"Could we say she's here as your companion?" Chas suggested.

Mrs Jackson cocked her head to one side. "She is a little young but ... perhaps we could say she's the daughter of friends and they've had to go overseas for a few months."

Ann felt invisible as Chas paced the room, a frown etched on his face.

"Yes, that could work."

"Nonsense." Mr Jackson interrupted. "Where on earth would they go with Napoleon wreaking havoc all over Europe?"

"He's concentrating on the Iberian peninsula at the moment," Chas said. "Most of France should be passable ... and most of the Germanic states by now."

Mrs Jackson wafted a hand in the air. "I'm sure we don't need to go into too much detail ... we could say they haven't told us where they've gone. Besides, I'm sure Elizabeth has no idea about what goes on outside of Birmingham, let alone England."

Mr Jackson attacked another currant bun. "You have a point, although I think we'll need a bit of detail. Let's go with France and onto Bern to take in the air in the mountains."

"That may work; they could spend an indefinite amount of time there." Chas turned to Ann. "Are you happy to say your parents are travelling and you're here as a companion to my aunt?"

"Yes ... I suppose so, but what does it mean to take the air?"

"Mountains, my dear." Mr Jackson wiped his mouth with a napkin. "Bern is a town in the mountains north of Italy. The Alps. The air there is supposed to be good for the constitution."

Ann nodded. "Very well. I should remember that. It won't be for long though, will it?"

"I hope not." Chas winked as he touched her fingers.

"I shall excuse you from your companioning while she's

here," Mrs Jackson said. "I'll tell her that she's enough of a companion for anyone. Will that do?"

Ann breathed a sigh of relief. "Yes, thank you. You're very kind."

Ann had retired to her new room to dress for dinner when she heard a commotion downstairs. She opened the door a crack to see that their visitors had arrived.

"Chas, come and sit with us," two excitable voices shrieked with delight.

"Where did you get your fancy clothes from?" one of them said. "You look different."

Ann didn't hear his reply as they disappeared down the hall towards the drawing room. *That must be Lucy and Rebecca.* They were the younger of the sisters if she remembered correctly but they didn't sound like the reserved young ladies she was expecting to meet.

"Did you have a good journey, Elizabeth?" Mrs Jackson was still in the hall.

"No, the journey was dreadful, far worse than I expected."

"Well, why did you put yourself through it?"

"Because I couldn't stay in Birmingham a moment longer. Charles had told me how comfortable he was here and so I thought that if he could come and hide down here, so could I."

Ann shrank back from the door. *Come and hide?* What was he hiding from ... and why hadn't he told her?

She straightened up and put her ear back to the door.

"At least a month, I would say. I couldn't face the journey back any sooner. You don't mind, do you?" The voices trailed off down the hall before the door to the drawing room closed.

They'll be here for a month? That's what it sounded like.

But what were they hiding from that they needed to be here for so long? She closed the bedroom door and perched on the end of the bed. Should she go down and join them or wait to be invited? It wasn't much of a decision and she wandered to a chair by the window that overlooked the back of the house. *What's Chas hiding?* He was always so kind and polite, although thinking about it, he had shouted at her a couple of times this week. *Why?* The first time was when she'd gone to meet Jane, she could understand that, he was worried ... but when she'd asked where they'd lived, why had that made him angry?

She stared out of the window as thoughts raced through her mind, but at some point she must have dozed off because the next thing she heard was footsteps running up the stairs and the door being thrown open.

"Oh!" An overly tall, thin girl with dark curls protruding from her plain white bonnet stood in the centre of the room. A smaller version stood behind her. "Who are you?"

Ann stood up, clutching her shawl to her chest. "Good afternoon, I'm Mrs Evans, a companion to Mrs Jackson."

"If you're her companion, why weren't you with her when we arrived?" A frown settled on the girl's face.

"She ... erm ... she said I wouldn't be required with there being so many visitors and so I came to change for dinner."

"In here?"

Ann could feel her cheeks flushing as the second girl stepped forward and linked an arm into her sister's.

"Mrs Jackson asked if I wouldn't mind sharing with you ... she wanted your mother to have my room while you're here."

"Did you say *Mrs* Evans?" the younger sister asked. "Doesn't your husband mind you being here?"

Ann pursed her lips. "I'm a widow. I moved back in with my parents when my husband died but they're travelling overseas ... to take the air ... and so Mrs Jackson suggested I come here."

"They've gone overseas? How exciting." The older girl spoke again. "Where've they gone?"

"I-I can't remember." Ann walked towards the door.

"Not to worry, we can study the globe later and see if it reminds you."

"Actually ... they might have mentioned France ... and something about being burned." Ann hesitated before she stepped onto the landing. "I'll go and leave you to settle in? You must be tired after your journey."

"You don't have to go," the younger girl said. "We only came up to see the room. We're going back down ourselves now. You can come with us if you want."

Ann looked from one sister to the other.

"You need to meet Mother and Eve and it would be as well to do it before dinner rather than skulking up here."

"I suppose so."

The elder girl held the door open. "In case you're wondering, I'm Lucy and this is Rebecca. So much easier than calling us both Miss Jackson." With a brief smile, Lucy walked through the door, leaving Rebecca to follow.

As soon as they entered the drawing room, Lucy and Rebecca hurried back to their places on the settee either side of Chas, but once he saw her, he stood up and offered her a chair.

"Mother, Eve, can I introduce Mrs Evans. She's staying here at the moment as a companion to Aunty."

Elizabeth rolled her eyes at Mrs Jackson. "What on earth

do you need a companion for? Don't you have enough visitors to keep you occupied?"

"In actual fact, Mrs Evans is a widow; she's here because her parents are away. We're being companions to each other."

"They've gone overseas." Lucy's eyes were wide. "Don't you think that's splendid?"

"France, she thinks, although she said they may be burned." Rebecca shuddered. "I'm not sure I'd like that."

"That's enough, girls; I'm sure Mrs Evans said nothing of the sort." Eve's lips curled into a smile.

"They've gone to Bern in the Alps to take the air." Chas shook his head. "And I thought you two had been to school."

"That's what she said..." Rebecca pointed to Ann, but Eve interrupted.

"I'm sorry we've intruded on your stay, Mrs Evans; I hope you'll be able to put up with us."

Ann's cheeks burned and she glanced at Chas before giving Eve her sweetest smile. "I'm sure I will."

"Marvellous," Mrs Jackson said. "I'm so glad I put you all together. It will do Mrs Evans good to have girls her own age to talk to."

CHAPTER SEVENTEEN

It had been a long time since Ann had shared a bed with anyone and she didn't remember ever sharing with a practical stranger. She rolled her head over the pillow to see the rounded shape of Eve alongside her, her breath still heavy with sleep. *At least Jane and Susan will have their own beds again.*

Over on the other side of the room, Lucy and Rebecca were whispering to each other, but she wasn't ready to bid them good morning. They'd been good enough company last night, but she couldn't help thinking they were hiding something from her.

She longed to speak to Chas, but his sisters flocked around him whenever he was in the room, making it impossible. He'd become quite distant too, or at least he was when his mother was around. *He has to tell her; I can't carry on like this for a month.* She was staring at the ceiling when a voice from beside her caused her to jump.

"Will you two stop whispering? I'd swear it's worse than

you having a full-blown conversation. At least that way I'm not trying to catch the occasional word."

"Well, wake up then, sleepy." Rebecca scrambled out of her bed and jumped onto theirs, giving no regard to whether Ann was awake or not."

"Hey." A second later Eve sat up. "Will you behave? We're not in Birmingham now; you need to start acting like young ladies for a change. You've woken Mrs Evans up."

Ann pulled herself up. "Please, call me Ann, and don't worry, I was already awake. I hope you slept well."

"Like a baby, or at least like a good baby who knows when its mother is worn out." Eve glared at her sisters. "Not that I remember any like that."

Ann chuckled. "You'll have seen quite a few babies over the years, I imagine."

"We all have," Lucy said. "Enough to put us off forever."

"Really? I always enjoyed looking after my sisters. I still do."

"How many?" Lucy didn't waste her words.

"Just the two now. Mother had two others, but they didn't make it."

A wistful look crossed Eve's face. "It's always terrible when that happens."

"And the more you have, the more likely you are to lose some." Lucy sat cross-legged on the bed and folded her arms in front of her. "Why can't women understand that?"

Ann's forehead puckered. "Surely you should have plenty of children so that if you lose any, you have others left?"

Lucy shook her head. "The more you have, the further the food has to go around, and the less attention you can give them. That's why more die."

Eve held her hands up. "That's enough." She turned to Ann. "Don't get her started on issues of wives and mothers. She's only seventeen but she's already decided that neither are for her. How she can possibly know at her age, I've no idea."

"So have I," Rebecca said.

Ann stared at them, her eyes wide. "But who'll look after you?"

The girls laughed.

"We will." Lucy rolled her eyes. "Me and Rebecca work for Eve and we're going to make sure we can take care of ourselves."

Ann's jaw dropped.

"I run a business in Birmingham," Eve said. "We're dealers in ready-made linen. It's been going so well I've had to give this pair a job."

"You'll be glad you did," Lucy said. "I've already found some new outlets for you."

"I helped..." Rebecca elbowed Lucy in the ribs.

"I've never heard of women running their own businesses before, not serious ones like that. Why do you do it when you'll be getting married?"

"So that we don't have to get married." Lucy's expression was sombre.

Eve sighed. "That's not the reason and you know it. I started it a few years ago when we needed the money. Father didn't leave us much when he died and there were a lot of us dependent on it."

"Didn't your mother want to remarry?"

Eve chuckled. "She did not. She'd had a hard enough life with Father and she wasn't going to go through it again."

"She's the reason I want to work," Rebecca said. "Men are too demanding and unreliable."

Ann climbed out of bed and walked to the window. "Not all men..."

"Well, all the men in our family..."

"That's enough!"

Ann spun around to see Eve glaring at Rebecca. "I won't hear a word against him. Come along, let's get dressed and Ann can show us around the area before breakfast."

By the time they returned from their walk, breakfast had been laid out in the drawing room. The two Mrs Jacksons had started, but Mr Jackson and Chas were nowhere to be seen.

"Where's Chas?" Rebecca asked.

"I've sent him to work with your uncle," Elizabeth said. "It's about time he did a full day's work instead of idling around here."

"But when will we see him? We wanted him to take us out this afternoon."

Exactly. Ann's stomach churned.

"You'll see him at dinner and be done with it." Elizabeth helped herself to a cake. "He's not just here to entertain you. Now, sit down and have something to eat."

Ann waited for the girls to sit down before she found herself a chair. She no longer had any appetite but accepted the hot chocolate Esther handed her.

"Where've you been anyway?" Elizabeth asked once they settled.

"Ann's shown us around the area. We walked down past St Paul's Cathedral towards the river. It's quite nice, but very windy once you get down there."

"Didn't you want to show them the market at Clerkenwell

Green?" Mrs Jackson asked Ann. "They may like to see where we get our fabric and accessories."

"No. I didn't think to." Ann sipped her drink.

"Oh, well you must. I'm sure Eve would be interested."

"Yes, indeed. There may even be fabric down here that we can't get at home. Shall we go this afternoon?"

"Oh..." Ann put a hand to her mouth as a wave of nausea passed over her. "Excuse me, I need to go..." Without waiting for a response, she stood up and left the room with as much dignity as she could. As soon as she reached the hall, she headed towards the back door, perspiration building on her forehead. She couldn't go to the market. Confound Elizabeth for sending Chas away.

The air was cold once she reached the back yard, but she gratefully inhaled several large breaths. After a minute, the nausea subsided, and she shivered.

"Are you all right?" Esther had followed her outside.

"I am now, thank you. I suddenly came over all queasy. I think perhaps I'll go for a lie down."

"I noticed you didn't eat any breakfast. Would you like me to bring you something up?"

"Perhaps later. Will you apologise to the girls for me? I'm sure Mrs Jackson could show them to the market."

Esther raised an eyebrow. "Are you sure? I wouldn't be certain she knows the way."

Ann remained in bed for the rest of the morning, praying that everyone would go out. When she finally heard the front door close, she relaxed before throwing off the covers and moving to the chair by the window. The sky was grey and the shrubs at the bottom of the narrow garden had no colour to distract her.

"A penny for your thought." Esther walked into the room carrying a hot chocolate and a tray of cakes. "These were left over from breakfast."

Ann smiled. "Thank you. What would I do without you?"

"You were deep in concentration. I don't suppose you even heard me knock on the door."

Ann put a hand to her chest. "Goodness, no I didn't." She sighed. "If you must know, I was thinking about Mr Chas. I really need to talk to him but either he's not here, or if he is, his sisters or mother are with him."

"Hasn't he told them about the two of you?"

"No." Ann gazed back out of the window. "For some reason, he's reluctant. I get the impression he's hiding something from me. You haven't heard anything have you?"

"Not really." Esther hesitated. "I did hear his mother ordering him off to work this morning though. She said something like, 'just because you can't work in Birmingham doesn't mean you can't work down here. You should be helping out your uncle to repay his generosity.'"

Ann's stomach fluttered, and she put down the cake she was about to bite into. "You got no sense of why he can't work in Birmingham?"

"No, none."

"And the girls haven't said anything?"

"I haven't spent much time with them."

Ann sighed. "No, I don't suppose you have. Rebecca said something last night about the men in the family being unreliable, but Eve stopped her before she said any more."

"That sounds very mysterious; you've roused my curiosity now. I'll make sure to keep my ears open."

Ann gave her a weak smile. "You will tell me if you hear anything, won't you?"

"You can rely on me, as long as you eat everything on that breakfast tray before I get back. I don't want to be responsible for you wasting away."

The light was fading fast when Ann heard the front door open and close. They were back. Seconds later, she heard the now familiar sound of Lucy and Rebecca racing up the stairs.

"Are you feeling better?" Lucy asked as she pushed open the door.

"A little, thank you."

"You still look peaky." Rebecca walked across the room towards her. "You should have come out with us and got some fresh air. That would have put some colour in your cheeks."

"I'm sure I'll be fine. I'll join you for dinner; that should help."

"I imagine it will, it's venison pie tonight." Lucy hung her cloak on the back of the door. "That would make anyone better."

"Why don't you come down now?" Rebecca said. "Cook's making us some hot chocolate to warm us up. I'm sure there'll be enough for you."

Ann eyed her companions. "I think I will." *And hopefully Chas will be back soon; that will certainly help.*

There was no sign of the men as they entered the drawing room, but Mrs Jackson was waiting.

"Oh good, you're here. How are you feeling?"

"A little better, thank you. Rebecca mentioned there'd be hot chocolate and I doubt there's anything that can't cure."

Mrs Jackson chuckled. "You're a quick learner, I'll give you that."

"What time will Chas be back?" Eve asked.

"Any time now. Mr Jackson likes to read the newspaper before dinner."

"Won't they join us in here?" Rebecca's face was pained.

"They will, but don't expect him to talk to us." Mrs Jackson rolled her eyes. "The world news takes priority at this time of day."

"Well, we'll have to make sure Chas doesn't take after him." Lucy moved to the edge of the settee. "He can sit here between me and Rebecca."

"I don't know what all the fuss is about." Elizabeth shifted in her seat. "We're here for at least the next month, you're going to see plenty of him."

At least! The blood drained from Ann's face. *Are they ever going to go home?*

Esther carried in the tray of hot chocolate and had no sooner finished pouring it than Chas and Mr Jackson joined them.

"You're here." Rebecca patted the empty space beside her. "Come and sit here with us."

Chas winked at Ann before he moved to the settee.

"Have you all had a nice day? Did Mrs Evans show you the delights of London?"

"She did this morning, but she wasn't well this afternoon."

"Not well?" Chas stopped to give her some attention. "Nothing serious I hope?"

"N-no. I just came over a little faint. I-I'm fine now."

His smile was brief. "Well, that's good. So, what did the rest of you do this afternoon?"

"We found a marvellous fabric stall at the market..." Eve

sat up straight to describe the linen they'd seen, but Chas's attention was fixed on Ann.

"So how did you find it if Mrs Evans wasn't with you?"

"I had to take them," Mrs Jackson said. "I haven't been down St John Street for years and now I remember why. Next time they can wait for Mrs Evans."

Chas turned back to his aunt. "Now they've been once, I'm sure they can take themselves again. They don't have to involve Mrs Evans in everything."

Rebecca tapped him on the back of the hand. "Don't be such a killjoy, she likes being with us ... don't you, Ann?"

"And I'm sure she'd enjoy looking at the material..."

"No!"

The room fell silent as they all stared at Chas.

"What I mean is, you can't assume she wants to do these things, she might prefer to stay here."

"Since when did you start speaking for her?" Elizabeth asked.

Chas stared at his mother. "I didn't ... but I know what you're like. Just let her make her own mind up rather than telling her what to do."

Ann's heart was pounding as Chas stood up and left the room. *I need to follow him...* She put down her cup and saucer. "Would you excuse me; I've come over all peculiar again." She fanned her hand in front of her face before she hurried across the room. Once she was in the hall with the door safely closed behind her, she stopped and paused for breath. *Where will he be?*

She made her way to the stairs but as she put her foot on the bottom step, she heard her name.

"In here."

With a quick glance around the hall, she rushed to the front room. As soon as she entered, Chas shut the door and pulled her close.

"Oh, my love, I'm so sorry you've had to deal with them all day."

"I couldn't go to the market with them…"

"Of course you couldn't."

She wrapped her arms around him. "I can't keep this pretence up for another month. Please, you have to tell them about us."

"I'll try but it's not that simple. Besides, Mother seems to want me out of the way."

Ann pulled herself from his embrace. "Is everything all right? Things feel different since they arrived."

He shook his head. "That's just my family for you."

"But I get the impression something's wrong."

A dark shadow passed over Chas's face. "What have they said?"

Ann bit down on her lip and walked over to the window. "Someone said you were hiding down here… Is that true?"

Chas's pause was a little too long. "No, it's not. It's just because I'm not in Birmingham. They can't find me whenever they want me."

"So there's nothing you're not telling me?"

He joined her by the window and pulled her to him. "Didn't we say we wouldn't have secrets from each other?"

Ann said nothing as she buried her head into his chest. *The money isn't really a secret. I'll tell him about it as soon as we're married.*

CHAPTER EIGHTEEN

With very little time left to change for dinner, Ann hurried up the stairs and went straight into the bedroom.

"Here she is," Rebecca said.

"Where've you been?" Lucy asked. "We expected you to be taking a lie down when we got back."

"I-I needed some air."

"With no hat and coat on?" Rebecca's eyes narrowed as she studied her, causing Ann to rub her hands up and down her arms.

"I came over all faint and was terribly warm. You said earlier that some fresh air would do me good and so I went into the back yard."

"I'd have thought you'd have cooled down a lot quicker than that."

"Leave the poor girl alone, she probably didn't want to be questioned by you two." Eve's smile was friendlier than those of her sisters. "And are you feeling better?"

Ann nodded. "Yes, thank you. I should be well enough to join you for dinner, as long as I can get myself changed."

"Here, let me help you." Eve took Ann's newly washed white dress from the hook on the wall. "Someone's been busy."

"Esther the maid's been very good to me. I don't know what I'd have done without her."

"We all need our allies."

With her clean dress on, Ann sat down by the mirror on the chest of drawers and took a brush to her hair. "I need to redo these curls. I think the damp ruined them this morning.

"Chas doesn't seem to mind." Rebecca put a hand over her mouth as she and Lucy chuckled to themselves.

"What do you mean?" Ann looked from Rebecca to Eve, the hairbrush still clutched over her head.

"Take no notice of them." Eve took the hairbrush from her and pulled it through her hair. "You two, behave yourselves or I'll make you eat your meal up here."

"But what do they mean?" Ann's eyes were wide. "What's he said?"

Eve sighed. "They saw Chas gazing over at you this afternoon."

"And you kept looking at him, too," Rebecca said. "Do you like him?"

"Well, yes, he's very nice, but..."

"And did he go outside with you?"

Ann's cheeks burned as she stared at Rebecca.

"Are you the reason he won't come home?"

Ann turned away. "He has been home. He's only just come back from Birmingham. I didn't see him for nearly four months."

A quizzical look crossed Lucy's face. "How long have you been here?"

"I ... erm ... I moved in just before he left, a couple of days earlier, if I remember rightly."

"How long did you say your parents would be away for?"

Ann's eyes flicked between each sister as they waited for an answer. "I-I don't think I did. They could be gone for up to half the year, they really weren't sure."

Eve put a hand on Ann's shoulder. "You know he has no money, don't you?"

Ann's brow furrowed as she stared at Eve's kindly face. "No money? Why would I know that? It would be of no concern to me."

"Well, in case it becomes your concern, let me warn you that he's in no position to marry you ... or anyone else for that matter. He was declared bankrupt at the end of last year and has numerous creditors in Birmingham waiting to be paid before he can do anything else."

"No!" Ann jumped from her seat. "That can't be true."

"Please, don't be angry with us." Eve took hold of her hands. "He's a wonderful man but we don't want you getting hurt. He should have told you."

"What is there to tell?"

Eve glanced at Lucy before she spoke. "He and Mother had a brassfounding business, making and selling brass goods, but our sister died towards the end of last year and Mother became distracted. She stopped paying the creditors but failed to mention it to Chas. He kept buying materials and before they knew it, the creditors were banging on the door for their money ... but they didn't have any."

Ann shook her head. She knew the part about his sister

was true. Did that mean the rest of it was, too? She stared at Eve, her eyes wide. "But he said we'd be married. Why would he lie about that?"

"Because he's trying to pretend it hasn't happened." Lucy's voice remained impassive as she sat on the bed. "It's also one of the reasons he won't come back to Birmingham unless he has to. It's easier for him to hide from his responsibilities when he's down here."

Ann shook her head. "I don't understand. Wouldn't he have been sent to the debtors' prison if he was a bankrupt?"

"He's fortunate. He'll be able to pay his debts and our uncle's being very generous. Don't let all his fancy clothes fool you; brassfounders don't normally dress like that. Our aunt insisted on buying them for him. They don't want anyone knowing the truth about him while he's staying with them."

"So all talk of us getting married was a lie?" Ann's voice was a whisper.

Eve pursed her lips as she held Ann's gaze. "I'm afraid it was, unless you happen to have money of your own."

Ann perched on the seat by the window as the girls scampered back downstairs. The bell would be rung for dinner shortly but how could she face Chas, knowing what she did now? Should she mention it to him, or carry on with the pretence of the marriage knowing she had the money to support them? At least he had no idea about that, which meant he wasn't marrying her for her money. How could he be? He loved her. And even if he was bankrupt, she loved him and should be there for him.

Gradually as the knot in her stomach released its grip, she settled back in the chair. If she could talk to him, perhaps tell him about the money, everything would be all right. The bell ringing for six o'clock roused her from her thoughts. She stood up and straightened her dress. She'd see if she could speak to him after dinner.

Chas and the girls were making their way to the dining room as Ann walked down the stairs and he looked up with a smile.

"Mrs Evans. I hope you're feeling better. Why don't you sit with me at dinner so I can keep an eye on you? I'm sure Lucy won't mind."

Lucy eyed her brother before glancing at Ann and giving a brief nod. "Just this once."

Chas extended his arm to Ann as he waited for her. "I'm glad all you girls are getting along so well. What do you have planned for tomorrow?"

Ann shrugged. "I don't think we have any plans ... unless we do and no one's told me."

"I'd love to go back to the fabric stall," Eve said as she took her seat next to Ann at the table.

"I don't think they open on a Saturday." Ann turned to Chas. "Do you know?"

Chas's eyes were like black dots. "No, they don't, and to be honest, I'd rather you didn't go down St John Street alone. It's not safe for women with all those cattle herders."

"It was all right the other day when we were together," Eve said. "You don't give us any credit for being able to look after ourselves."

"And you underestimate the danger." Chas's voice was stern. "Now, I won't hear any more about it; I don't want you going to the market unless I'm with you."

"You won't be going near any markets," Elizabeth said

from across the table. "Men are expected to be at work, and that includes you."

"Thank you, Mother, I'm well aware of that." A muscle in Chas's jaw twitched. "All I'm saying is that I'd rather the girls were escorted if they go to the market."

"I'm sure a walk along the river would be pleasant, even if it is cold." Mrs Jackson's breezy tone managed to reduce the tension in the room. "As long as you wrap up well."

"Won't you come with us?" Ann asked.

"Oh gracious, no. Elizabeth and I have some visiting we need to do. I'm sure you'll have a much better time without us."

Ann returned her attention to her pâté, but immediately stopped and held her breath as Chas slipped his hand onto the top of her leg. A thrill shot through her and she peeked at him from under her lowered eyelids.

"Have you heard much from your parents, Mrs Evans?"

The sound of her name jolted Ann back to her senses and she looked across the table to Elizabeth. "I'm sorry?"

"Have you heard from your parents? They've been gone quite a few months now I believe. Have they written to tell you of their whereabouts?"

Ann's cheeks coloured although whether it was because of Elizabeth's question or the fact that Chas was stroking her thigh with his thumb, she wasn't sure. "No ... no, they haven't. Mother doesn't write..."

"Really?" Elizabeth raised an eyebrow. "What about your father, he must, surely?"

"I imagine he's rather busy at the moment."

"Can you write?" Rebecca leaned across the front of Chas to Ann.

Ann's voice became a whisper. "I didn't go to school."

"Well, the sooner the Church of England adopts the same values as the Quakers the better. All girls would go to school if we had any say in the matter."

"Please, let's not start on that again." Mrs Jackson placed a hand on her sister-in-law's arm. "You know it's not going to happen."

"All I'm saying is that the established church has no consideration for women. Leaving the church was the best thing I ever did, and it would help a lot more women if they did likewise."

With no desire to join a conversation about the church, Ann focussed on her food. Chas had been distracted by the conversation and removed his hand and she found herself wishing he would reach out for her again.

"Are we going to play some games tonight?" Rebecca asked as the dessert plates were tidied away.

"What would you like to play?" Chas asked. "Mrs Evans, do you have a favourite game?"

"No, I can't say I do."

Elizabeth returned her attention to Ann. "Do you play an instrument, Mrs Evans?"

Ann's cheeks flushed again. "Not very well. I started to learn the pianoforte when I was young but haven't played for many years now."

"What a shame. Why did you stop?"

Telling everyone that her life had turned upside down when her father died wasn't an option. "My husband and I lived modestly; we didn't have room for a piano."

"Oh, the perils of marrying young. Did you have any children?"

Ann didn't know where to look. "No, we didn't."

"Very fortunate for you. I had my first son exactly nine months after I was married."

"Elizabeth!" Mrs Jackson's cheeks were scarlet. "That's hardly talk for the dinner table. Come along, let's go through to the drawing room and sort some games out."

Ann hesitated as the family stood up and headed for the door.

"What's the matter?" Chas whispered as he stood behind her waiting to help her from her seat.

Once Elizabeth left the room, she turned to face him. "You have to tell her about us, please. I feel so awkward..."

"I will, I promise, but it could cause more problems than it solves. Things really are better this way."

Ann bit down on her lip. "I told the girls about us earlier."

Chas's eyes narrowed. "What on earth did you do that for? Have you any idea what you've done. They'll tell Mother, of course."

"They gave me no choice, they guessed that we had feelings for each other."

Chas turned away in frustration. "How on earth did they guess? You must have hinted to them."

"Please Chas, I didn't. You have to believe me and despite what they said, I still want to marry you."

Chas turned back and stared at her. "What did they say?"

"Just that..." She took a deep breath. "Just that, you'd had a few problems in Birmingham, which was why you came down here."

"They had no right to say anything." He strode to the door and stormed out.

"Chas, come back, I don't mind..."

The front door slammed before she could reach him and she stopped to rest her head on the door frame. *What have I done?*

She closed her eyes and took a deep breath.

"There you are. Are you feeling sick again?" Esther walked towards her down the hall. "I thought you were feeling better when you were eating dinner."

"Oh, Esther. I don't know that I'll ever feel better. Not while Mr Chas's family are here."

Esther walked into the dining room to collect the dishes from the table. "They are rather overpowering. They won't be here forever though."

A wave of nausea swept over her. "Let's hope not. I think I'll retire for the evening. I really can't face any parlour games tonight. Can you send my apologies if anyone misses me?"

CHAPTER NINETEEN

The light was barely penetrating the drapes when Ann was woken by Lucy and Rebecca giggling on the other side of the room.

"What are you two doing?" Eve sat up, the sleepiness still evident in her voice.

"Nothing, just talking."

"Well, can you do it more quietly? You've woken me up and I'm sure you must have woken Ann, too."

Ann said nothing. She'd been awake for what felt like hours in the middle of the night but must have fallen asleep as the sun rose. She didn't have the energy to join a conversation.

"Are you really awake, Ann?" Rebecca's voice was loud enough to wake her even if she had been asleep.

"No."

'Yes you are." Rebecca jumped on the bed and found a spot to sit. "What happened to you last night? We thought you were going to join us. Did you go out with Chas?" She giggled.

"That's enough." Eve's tone was harsh.

"I was only asking. We waited for her."

Ann pushed herself up with a groan. "No, I didn't. He went by himself."

"Where to?"

"I don't know."

"Well, why didn't you join us?"

"Because I didn't feel like playing games." The sharpness in Ann's voice softened when Rebecca's face fell. "I'm sorry. If you must know, he was angry that I'd told you he'd asked me to marry him."

Eve took Ann's hand. "I'm sorry too. Did you tell him you knew about the bankruptcy?"

"Not in so many words, but he knew. I think that was what upset him the most."

"Men and their pride." Eve shook her head. "Someone like Chas should know better."

"Is that why you were in bed when we came upstairs?" Rebecca asked.

Ann nodded. "I was in bed, but I wasn't asleep. I just needed to be on my own."

Lucy came and perched on the edge of the bed. "We're telling you this for your own good. You really would be better off without him. He'll bring you nothing but trouble."

There were tears in Ann's eyes. "I don't want to be without him."

Eve patted her hand before she got out of bed. "Come on, let's get dressed and we can go for a walk."

Ann twisted the front of her nightdress. "Can you find your own way...? I was hoping to talk to Chas before he left for work."

"We need to talk first," Eve said. "If you're still set on marrying him, we need to tell you the truth."

"I can ask Chas…"

"And be told nothing?" Eve raised an eyebrow. "Trust me, he's still denying there's a problem; he won't tell you."

Ann sighed. "All right, but can I say good morning to him at least? I need to know he's not still angry with me."

"If you must, but let's be quick so we can be back in time for breakfast."

Ann used the washstand first and changed into her grey dress before reaching for her cloak. "I'm hoping he'll be in the front room and so I'll wait for you in the hall when he's gone."

Ann stepped out onto the landing in time to hear the door to the front room close. *That must be him.* A smile flickered on her lips and she hurried down the stairs. She was about to knock when she heard voices inside. *Elizabeth?*

"You most certainly will not marry her. Have I taught you nothing?"

"Mother, I'm twenty-six years old. I'll decide who I marry."

"Not if they're an outsider. You know very well you'd have to marry in a Church of England church and that's out of the question."

"It's not out of the question…"

"So you're prepared to go into a church and be disowned by your own kind after everything your father and I have done for you?"

"After everything you've done for me?" Chas was shouting now. "If it hadn't been for you, the business wouldn't have gone bankrupt."

"Me! I did everything I could to help you…"

Ann jumped at the sound of a hand hitting the table.

"When it was too late. You were the one who didn't pay the bills."

"That business was as much mine as yours. I did everything I could to stop the creditors pushing for bankruptcy."

"Well, clearly not enough."

"At least I stayed around to deal with the consequences, unlike you, running down here. Have you told Mrs Evans you're a bankrupt? See how much she likes you when you tell her ... and when she sees you out of these fancy London clothes."

"It's none of her concern."

There was a pause and Ann wondered what had happened before Elizabeth's voice rose.

"None of her concern? I can't believe I'm hearing this from my own son. If you can't put a roof over her head, then it most certainly is her concern."

"Uncle George has said we can stay here until the creditors are paid ... besides, she has money."

Ann felt as if she'd been punched in the stomach. *How does he know that?* She moved back to the stairs, the voices now distant as her ears buzzed. *He's been using me. He only wants me for the money.* She climbed the first couple of steps before sitting down, her head floating. A moment later she fell onto the wall and remembered nothing else.

How long she lay there she had no idea, but she was roused when the front door slammed. *What was that?*

In an instant, the conversation came flooding back but she was distracted as Rebecca hurried down the stairs.

"What was that? Ann, whatever's the matter?"

Ann propped herself up onto one elbow and wiped the perspiration from her face. "I-I think I fainted."

"Eve, Lucy, come down here, quickly."

Before Ann could focus her eyes, Elizabeth appeared at the bottom of the stairs. "What's going on here?"

"Oh Mother, thank goodness you're here." There was relief in Rebecca's voice. "It's Mrs Evans, she fainted. We need to get her upstairs."

"I'm coming." Eve hurried towards her. "Let me help."

Between Elizabeth and Eve, they got Ann to the bedroom and onto the bed.

"What brought that on?" Lucy stood at the foot of the bed, the usual unfathomable expression on her face.

"I-I don't know. I didn't sleep well last night. I'm probably tired."

"Well, I suggest you leave her to rest," Elizabeth said. "She doesn't need everyone fussing around her if she needs to sleep."

"Someone should sit with her though," Eve said. "You three go downstairs and I'll stay with her."

Eve waited for the bedroom door to close before she sat on the edge of the bed. "What happened?"

Ann couldn't stop her tears as she remembered the conversation. "He doesn't love me."

"Did you speak to him?"

She shook her head as garbled words escaped through her sobs. "He was talking to your mother. He only wants me for my money."

Eve paused. "You've got money?"

"I wish I didn't; it's caused more trouble than it's worth. It's the only reason people like me."

"Don't be silly, I'm sure that's not true. Did you tell Chas about it before he proposed marriage to you?"

"No, I haven't told him about it at all..."

"Well, there you are, it can't be the reason he wants to marry you."

Ann's sobs stopped as she stared at Eve. "But he knows... How did he find out if I didn't tell him?"

"Could anyone else have told him?"

Ann shook her head. "I didn't think so, but ... someone must have. He must have known before we even met. Why else would he have approached me when I was outside the house one day?"

Eve said nothing but stroked Ann's head as she buried her face in the pillow.

"He's taken me for a fool..."

Eve sighed. "I don't know what to say. It doesn't sound like him, but the bankruptcy has upset him."

Mustering all her strength, Ann rolled over and wiped her eyes before swinging her legs out of bed. "I need to leave."

"Where will you go?"

Ann sniffed. "I'll have to go back to Mother's and admit she was right all along."

Eve cocked her head to one side and raised an eyebrow. "I thought she was travelling?"

Ann gulped in some air. "That was a story we made up. Mother didn't want me to marry Chas. She said he only wanted me for my money, and I was adamant that he didn't. We argued and I left..."

"Oh Ann, I'm so sorry."

"So am I, but at least my sisters will be pleased to see me." She stood up.

"What about your clothes? Do you have a bag to put them in?"

Ann gaped at the clothes hanging on the wall. "Your aunt lent them to me. She's been so kind, I really should thank her before I go, but..."

"But what?"

"I can't face your mother, not after what she said about me; and they're likely to be together. Will you thank your aunt for me ... and Esther? I wouldn't have managed without her."

Eve stood up and shook her head. "No, you must do that. Let me go and distract Mother and you can say your farewells."

Half an hour later, Ann walked down Compton Street towards St John Street. The wind was bitter, and she longed to be indoors, but what sort of reception would she get? Her mother would probably be in the scullery making bread, but she had no idea where Jane and Susan would be. *If I could only speak to them first.*

She got to the corner of Compton Street and stopped. Jane may be at the market. Should she wait for her? She was in no hurry to go home, so why not? She moved to the side of the footpath, studying everyone who passed. The last time she was here, she'd been with Chas. This was their corner. She moved a little further along. This was the spot where he'd kissed her, when Father Jacobs had seen them together. She couldn't stay here either.

She turned and headed towards Clerkenwell Green. It didn't matter where she stood, she'd be able to find Jane. She stopped to study the faces around her. What if she'd missed her? She'd no idea what time it was, or even when Jane went out if she had other chores to do. The now familiar feeling of sickness returned to her stomach and she closed her eyes. *Just be patient.*

Her feet were cold, and she shifted from one foot to the other as she blew into her hands to warm them, but it was no use; she'd have to go and face her mother alone.

She turned and headed back up the street, the wind worsening the tears that were already in her eyes. *What if she won't have me?* She felt the money bag attached to the waistband of her petticoat. *No, that won't be a problem.* But what about the scolding she was likely to get? She stopped. She couldn't do it. With her heart racing, she glanced around. Where else could she go?

A tavern across the road caught her eye. She'd never been in before, but surely they'd let her have a room if she had the money. Her heart was pounding. It would mean admitting she had some money. *Confound the money; I was better off without it.* As a couple of drovers brought up the rear of a herd of cattle, she stepped out into the road but stopped as a cheer rose from the other side of the street. The tavern had just opened for the day and a group of men who'd been waiting outside filed in. No, she couldn't go yet; let them get their ale first. She turned around once more to be greeted by the most beautiful sight in the world.

"Jane!" With tears now spilling down her cheeks she ran to her sister, who was making her return from the market.

"Ann, oh my dear, whatever's the matter?"

Jane dropped her basket as the two of them threw their arms around each other.

"I need to come home." Ann sobbed onto her sister's shoulder.

"What's happened to Mr Jackson? I thought you were to be married."

Ann wiped her eyes and straightened up. "Not any more. Oh Jane, I've been such a fool, but the worst part is, Mother was right. I can't face the thought of going home if she's going to do nothing but tell me what a dunderhead I've been."

"She won't do that, honestly she won't. She's missed you."

Missed the money more likely. "I don't know why. She never had a civil word to say to me while I was at home."

"The way you left shocked her. She didn't expect you to go. Come back with me now. I think you'll be surprised."

"Very well; I haven't anywhere better to go." Ann wiped her face and allowed Jane to link her arm as they walked the last hundred yards home.

CHAPTER TWENTY

A nn hovered outside the front door as Jane went into the house. This was it. She put her foot on the front step, the step she'd been cleaning when Chas had first spoken to her. Had he really known about her money all those months ago? She remembered the first time she'd seen him. How could he possibly have known? *He thought I was the maid!*

"Ann. Is that you?" She flinched at the sound of her mother's voice. "Are you back?"

Ann trudged up the steps, her head bowed. "I'm sorry, I've been such a fool. Will you forgive me?"

Mrs Davies raised her hands in the air. "Praise the Lord."

Ann saw a hint of a smile on her mother's face.

"Father Jacobs said you'd be back."

"Father Jacobs?" Ann's forehead creased.

"Don't look like that, of course, Father Jacobs. He's prayed with me every day for your safe return. Wait until I tell him." Mrs Davies put an arm around Ann's shoulders. "Now, don't just stand there, come inside."

With the front door shut, Mrs Davies escorted her into the living room.

"Susan, come and see who's here."

Jane watched from the scullery while Susan ran towards Ann and threw her arms around her.

"Where've you been? We've all been sad without you."

She wrapped her arms around Susan's shoulders. "I've not been far, but I'm back now. I've missed you."

"Jane, boil some water so we can have a cup of tea while Ann tells us what she's been doing." Mrs Davies pointed to a chair. "Where have you been? We've been worried about you … and what have you done with Mr Jackson?"

"I've left him." She sat down and put her head in her hands. "You were right, he only wanted me for the money. Not that he admitted it; I overheard him talking to his mother about me."

Mrs Davies shook her head. "You've got a lot to learn about men, my girl, in fact, you all have. They'll tell you anything until they get a wedding ring on your finger and then everything changes."

"But how will we ever know who to marry?" There was concern in Jane's voice.

"You bring him home and get my approval … and no Quakers or Methodists."

"But that will rule out half the men…"

"Jane dear, do you want to be like Ann? When you leave here, I want it to be with the right man and with my blessing."

Ann bit her tongue. Why couldn't her mother see the world was changing? Not that there was any point arguing. She didn't want to leave home again.

"What's the point of going to listen to the Methodist

preachers then?" Jane stomped off back to the scullery for the tea.

"I would hope that you go to listen to the sermons, not to associate with young men."

"I do." Jane returned with a tea tray of cups and saucers. "But if you don't mind us listening to them, why can't we marry one of them? It makes no sense."

"Listening to a sermon and being married to a dissenter are two very different things. Now, go and get the teapot before Ann tells us what she's been doing."

Ann was exhausted by the time she went up to bed that night. Her mother may have allowed them half an hour to talk over a cup of tea, but it hadn't stopped her reorganising the chores. She had only been gone for six days but she had quite got out of the habit of doing anything strenuous.

"How are you feeling?" Jane propped herself up on one elbow as Ann sat on the edge of her bed.

Ann shook her head. "Being back here it's as if the last week didn't happen."

"It must have been nice to have your own maid."

Ann thought of Esther. "Yes, it was. She was a nice girl too."

"Well, at least you can stop putting on airs. I don't know how you did it."

Ann swung her legs into bed. "It wasn't too bad ... except when Chas's mother was there. I got the impression she thought she was better than she was, but the others were all lovely. Apart from not seeing Chas, I'm mostly sorry I won't see his sisters."

"Well, tuck yourself into bed and we'll go out tomorrow. I

think there's another preacher here, so we can go and listen to him."

Ann grinned at her sister. "Only as long as you promise not to eye any of the young men."

Despite the lateness of the year, daylight was filtering through the drapes when Ann woke the following morning. She lay still staring at the ceiling wondering if she'd just woken from a vivid dream. She studied Jane and Susan as they slept before creeping from the room and down the stairs so as not to wake them.

She brought in the meat that had been stored on the cold slab by the back door and set about scrubbing the potatoes for dinner. It was the least she could do to repay them for the extra chores they'd taken on while she'd been away. She had almost finished when her mother appeared in the doorway.

"You're up early."

"I just wanted to get this done for you. Jane and Susan are still asleep. I think they're exhausted after everything they've had to do. Did you have to get rid of the maid again?"

Mrs Davies bustled past her to put some water on to boil. "I'm not made of money. If I don't watch the pennies, they'll soon run out. You've run your own house; you should know that."

Ann nodded. "I do; I just wish you could find a way to make a bit of extra money for yourself. I won't be here forever."

"A shilling a week wouldn't go amiss, especially not with all that money you've got." Mrs Davies straightened herself up. "Then we could get a maid."

Ann picked up the pot of meat and potatoes and placed it by the small fire. "You're right, I shouldn't have left you with nothing. Why don't you get another maid and I'll pay for her?"

Once her mother had left for church, Ann clambered back upstairs and took over from Susan as she helped Jane make the beds.

"Has she gone?" Jane asked.

"She has, no doubt to give thanks that my heart's been broken."

"I'm sure she's not; she's been really nice to you since you came back ... in fact she's even been nice to me and Susan."

Ann tucked the blankets under the corner of the bed. "I must admit, she surprised me yesterday but I suppose I should be grateful. She's agreed to get another maid, too."

Jane beamed across the bed. "I'm so glad you're back."

"And I'm glad it's Sunday," Ann said. "After everything I had to do yesterday, I need a day off."

Jane chuckled. "Having your own maid has been the ruin of you. You need to come back to reality."

"I'm sure that won't take long."

"Are we going to listen to the preacher this afternoon?" Jane asked as they moved over to the second bed.

"I don't see why not; it's a nice enough day."

"Well, if we get washed up after breakfast in good time, perhaps we can leave early. Walk the long way around."

"Are you going to sneak off again?" Susan asked.

"No, not today." Ann sighed. "Maybe not ever."

"Stop that." Jane flicked Ann's arm. "Now come on, let's get this table set."

The breakfast was on the table by the time Mrs Davies returned and Ann seated Susan at the table while Jane made a pot of tea. Mrs Davies helped herself to a currant bun.

"Father Jacobs says there's a preacher again this afternoon. He's asked me to go with him to see what all the talk is about."

Ann stiffened. "And you're going?"

"Why shouldn't I?"

"Why shouldn't you?" Ann's eyes widened. "The man tried to swindle us and you're planning on walking out with him."

"Don't be silly; it's nothing of the sort. He knows I'm familiar with their sermons and so thought I'd be a good companion for his first visit. If he wants to go again, I imagine he'll ask someone else."

"Oh."

"What's the matter, don't you want us to come?"

"I'm sure I don't mind you coming, but Father Jacobs ... well, shall we just say I hope he doesn't think he's getting any more money off me just because he prayed for me to come back."

"I'm sure the thought won't have crossed his mind; he's a very forgiving man. It would be nice if you could be civil to him though."

Jane placed the teapot in the middle of the table. "Who are you being civil to?"

Ann rolled her eyes. "Mother and Father Jacobs are going to listen to the preacher this afternoon."

Jane spun her head to face Ann. "Are they walking out together?"

"Will you two stop this? No, we're not walking out together, we just happen to be walking to St John's together. He's picking me up at half past one."

Jane's shoulders slumped. "We were going to leave as soon as we've tidied up here. Can we meet you there?"

"If you must, but I'll be watching the pair of you." She eyed Ann and Jane.

"I'm sure there'll be nothing to see."

Once they'd finished eating, Susan went to fetch the cloaks, while Ann and Jane washed the dishes. As soon as they were ready, they set off down St John Street.

"I expect it'll be busy today." Jane linked her arm through Ann's, while Susan held onto Ann's other hand. "It's a good job we're early,"

"I suppose so. Can you believe it was only this time last week I was here with Mr Williams?" Ann stopped abruptly and stared at her sister. "You don't think he'll be here, do you?"

"He wasn't very happy when he was here last week," Susan said.

Ann bit her lip. "No, you're right, he wasn't."

"Wasn't that because me and Susan were with you?"

"That was part of it, but he doesn't like the Methodists either."

Jane patted her hand. "Well, there you are then. He's not likely to come and listen of his own accord, is he?"

Ann relaxed. "You're right. It would be the last place he'd want to be."

Despite walking the long way around, the square outside St John's Church was quiet when they arrived. Jane pointed to a space to one side where they could perch on a small shelf in the wall.

"Why don't we go over there? It will save our feet for the walk home."

"We must be early," Ann said. "It's not as busy as I thought it would be.

"Perhaps people have gone to the river instead with it being such a pleasant day for the time of the year."

Ann nervously eyed those who were already there as they walked across the square. "I wonder if we shouldn't have done that too."

"Are you all right?"

"I don't know. Now we're here, I can't help worrying that Mr Williams will turn up. Would you mind if we left?"

"What about Mother? She'll be watching out for us."

Ann sighed. "I'd forgotten about her. Why's she so keen to come?"

Jane shrugged. "She has been threatening to for weeks."

Ann sighed. "Do you think Father Jacobs could have seen me by the river on one of the Sundays I told her I was coming here? I did think he'd been following us a few months ago."

"You're being paranoid; of course that's not why she's coming. You've told her you're not seeing Mr Jackson any more."

Ann's eyes were wide. "What if she didn't believe me? What if she thought I only said it so I could come home?"

"And leave a life of luxury with your own maid? I don't think so."

Ann tried to control her breathing. "Yes, you're right. I'd still like to go though. If she misses us, we could tell her that we took a walk along the river and didn't realise the time."

The square was filling up, and as they reached the far side a chill ran down Ann's spine.

"Mrs Evans, is that you?"

Ann turned to see Mr Williams staring down at her. "Mr

Williams ... g-good afternoon." She clung to Jane's arm, refusing to let her leave. "I didn't expect to see you here; you said the Methodists weren't for you."

There was no smile on his face. "They're not. I came to see you."

"Me?" Ann's voice squeaked. "How did you know I'd be here?"

"I didn't, but I hoped you would be ... on your own." He glared at Jane.

"Oh ... well, as you can see, I have my sisters with me."

A muscle in his cheek twitched as he eyed the three of them. "You misunderstand me. I want to speak to you alone."

Ann's heart missed a beat. "I don't think that's a good idea. There's really nothing to say."

He took hold of her free arm. "I beg to differ. You ran off last week without a word..."

"The lady said she didn't want to talk to you."

Ann spun around to see Chas standing behind her, but he said nothing as he stepped around her and came face to face with Mr Williams. "Leave her alone." He pushed Mr Williams on the shoulder causing him to stumble backwards.

"Get off me." Mr Williams regained his footing and pushed him back. "All I want to do is talk."

"She's already spoken for. Now get out of here." Chas pulled back his right arm, his fist clenched, but Ann grabbed hold of it.

"Stop, both of you. I've nothing to say to either of you, just leave us alone."

Mr Williams glowered at Chas. "So, she doesn't want you, either? In that case, what right have you to keep her from me?"

Chas put his face to within an inch of Mr Williams's. "I have every right because she's going to be my wife."

"Not if I've got anything to do with it." Mr Williams pushed Chas to one side and took hold of Ann's arm. "She wants nothing to do with you."

Chas leapt forward to release her, but Mr Williams was too quick and pushed him away causing him to fall backwards.

"Stop this!" Ann wrenched her arm from Mr Williams's grasp. "I'll speak for myself and I don't want anything to do with you."

A crowd began to circle around them as Chas staggered to his feet and lunged towards Mr Williams. He struck him firmly in the stomach but before he could aim another punch, Mr Williams hit back with a right hook to the jaw. Chas crashed back into the crowd, blood seeping from the cut.

"Stop this." Ann pushed Susan out of the way before she stepped between them, but Jane held her back.

"Let's just go. You don't want to see either of them again."

"No, you go ... take Susan..." Her words were cut short as Chas hurled himself at Mr Williams, knocking him to the ground. He jumped on top of him, his fist raised, but Mr Williams rolled to one side and threw himself onto Chas, pinning him to the floor.

"Get off him!" Ann grabbed at Mr Williams's shoulder, but he shrugged her out of the way before he landed a punch on Chas's cheek.

"Stop! Someone, stop them ... he'll kill him." She pushed Mr Williams from the side and deflected a shot that was heading for Chas's temple. A second later two men appeared from the crowd and pulled Mr Williams away, leaving Chas lying bloodied and injured on the floor.

Ann immediately knelt down beside him and ran a finger over his cheek.

"Let me finish him off." Mr Williams kicked at those around him but Ann glared up at him before speaking to his captors.

"Take him away from me, as far away as you possibly can. I never want to see him again."

Chas tried to sit up. "Let me at the scoundrel. I'll finish him off."

Ann put an arm around his shoulders and eased his head onto her lap. "You'll do nothing of the sort." She took a handkerchief from her pocket. "Let me clean you up first and then I'll walk you home."

Chas's mouth curled into a smile as he stared up at Mr Williams.

"I'll get you..." Mr Williams broke free from one of his captors but froze when a shrill voice cut through the noise.

"What on earth's going on here?" Mrs Davies's eyes were like slits as she surveyed the scene.

"Mother!" Ann jumped up. "I-it's not what it looks like..." Her eyes flicked around those standing closest to her. "There was a misunderstanding."

"I'd say it was rather more than that; now, get yourself home this minute. I'll deal with you there."

"No." Ann's cheeks burned as she held her mother's gaze. "I'm not letting Mr Jackson walk home in this condition. I'm going to help him."

"You'll do no such thing."

"I will..."

Mrs Davies turned as Father Jacobs appeared from out of the crowd, a smug grin appearing on his face.

"I told you she was still seeing him."

"I wasn't still seeing him and for your information, a lot of what's gone on this last week has been entirely your fault."

Mrs Davies grabbed Ann's arm. "Where are your manners? I didn't bring you up to speak to Father Jacobs like that."

With a shrug, Ann pulled her arm free. "I'll speak to him any way I like because he's nothing but a charlatan. He's followed me around for months and threatened to report back to you if I wouldn't give him the tithe he wanted. He should be ashamed of himself."

A gasp echoed around her and she nodded to the crowd. "See! Everyone else thinks so, too."

The jowl under Father Jacobs's chin shook as he spluttered. "I did no such thing. I was protecting her."

"You were protecting nobody but yourself. You tried to get some money from me but when you had no success with me, you turned to Mother. If I'm not mistaken, I'd say this friendship you're encouraging is nothing more than a ruse so you can ask for her hand in marriage and get the money that way?"

"Don't be ridiculous." Mrs Davies stood tall, but the colour drained from her face as she turned to face the priest. "Don't tell me she's right. How could you? I trusted you…"

"So did I once." Ann moved to her mother's side. "But you reminded me that the love of money is the root of all evil and that some have erred from the faith because of it. It looks like you've been as gullible as I was."

Father Jacobs's ruddy cheeks glowed as he spluttered. "I will not stand here and listen to this ... this nonsense."

"And neither will I. I've had enough of being told what to do and one day I'll marry whoever I choose." Ann turned her back on her mother and knelt down beside Chas, who had propped himself up onto one elbow.

"Is he still here?" He stared up at Mr Williams. "I think the lady said she wanted you gone."

Mr Williams had stopped struggling while Ann had been speaking but he kicked out at those around him as he was pulled through the crowd. They could still hear him shouting as the preacher arrived on the makeshift stage at the other side of the square. As he began the opening prayer, the crowd moved back to their original positions.

Jane crouched down beside Ann. "Is he all right?"

Ann's heart pounded as she ran a finger over the swelling around his left eye. "I don't know."

"I will be—" he winced as he changed position "—if you take care of me."

"But you can't..." Jane's eyes were wide. "You promised."

Chas ignored Jane. "Why did you leave?"

Ann glanced up at the uncompromising eyes of her mother before she threw her arms around Chas's neck. "I don't know. I really don't know."

CHAPTER TWENTY-ONE

The sermon had started by the time Ann helped Chas to his feet.

"Can you manage?"

Chas winced as he put his weight on his left leg.

"Yes, he can." Mrs Davies took hold of Susan's hand as she glared at him. "I've never seen anything so disgraceful in my life ... and embarrassing Father Jacobs like that, too."

The tears had disappeared from Ann's eyes. "Father Jacobs brought it on himself ... and so did you. You told me you had no intention of marrying again."

"I haven't–" Mrs Davies's voice softened "–but sometimes a little attention is nice..."

"Well, he was using you to get to me..."

Chas linked his arm through hers. "Come along, arguing will only make things worse. You don't want to say something you'll regret."

Mrs Davies stepped forward. "If you go home with him..."

"...I'll be back in time for dinner. We'll talk then, but I've told you, I'll make my own decisions from now on."

"But you can't." There were tears in Jane's eyes.

Ann rested her hand on her sister's arm. "I have to talk to Mr Jackson. I left him without a word and he at least needs an explanation."

"That was all Mr Williams wanted."

"Maybe he did, but everything changed when Mr Williams did this." Ann ran a hand down the side of Chas's face. "I know what I want now." She watched as her mother grabbed Susan's hand and stormed away, before turning back to Jane. "I'll see you at home. I promise."

Chas put an arm on Ann's shoulder as they watched Jane hurry to catch up with Mrs Davies. "Come on, I need to find somewhere to sit. I think that blockhead's done something to my leg as well."

"I'm sorry." For the first time that afternoon, tears pricked her eyes. "That should never have happened, I'll never forgive myself if he's damaged you."

Chas stroked her hand. "It wasn't your fault..."

They kept their thoughts to themselves as they struggled towards St Paul's Cathedral.

"There's a bench against the wall over there. "Ann pointed towards a seat nestled in a corner between two white stone walls. She helped him sit down before she perched next to him. "I'm sorry for what happened..."

He held her hands as his swollen eye closed over. "So, tell me the truth, why did you leave? You must have had a reason, but Eve wouldn't tell me."

"No, I don't suppose she would." Ann took a deep breath. "Do you love me?"

Chas's brows drew together. "Of course I do; isn't it obvious?"

"Not when you lied to me."

"Lied? I didn't lie."

"What about the bankruptcy? Eve had already mentioned it, but you wouldn't talk to me about it, and then I overheard you and your mother arguing. Why didn't you tell me?"

"I was going to..."

"Once you'd got your hands on my money?"

Chas stopped, his confusion evident even through his bruised features. "Your money?"

"I heard you tell your mother that I had money. How did you know?"

"I-I didn't. I only said that to stop her arguing."

It was Ann's turn to look confused. "Why would you do that if you thought I was penniless?"

Chas let out a deep sigh. "All right, I guessed you probably weren't poor. If your late husband's family had a business at the docks, I imagined they had some money and it wasn't beyond the realms of possibility that you'd been left a legacy."

"And so you thought you'd marry me, take my money and get yourself out of trouble?"

Chas started to shake his head but a pained expression stopped him. "No, it wasn't like that. In fact, if you have got money, it could make things worse, not better."

"How?" Ann rubbed her forehead.

"If my creditors learn that I've come into money, they'd want to take it from me. I wouldn't want that."

"But that still doesn't explain why you didn't tell me you were bankrupt in the first place."

Chas hung his head over his lap. "It's hardly the first thing a man tells the woman he wants to marry."

"But we've known each other for months. Eve said the reason you went back to Birmingham over the summer was because you were summoned to court. Why didn't you tell me then?"

"Because I was frightened you wouldn't wait for me. You nearly didn't as it was." He touched the blood that had dried over the cut on his chin. "Is that why you left? Because I've been declared bankrupt."

Ann shook her head. "No, it was because I thought you only wanted me for my money."

"Oh Ann." He reached out and pulled her to him. "The idea hadn't even entered my mind. I want you for you. Why didn't you tell me about the money sooner? Do you have a lot?"

"Enough." Ann stood up and paced in front of him. "When I learned of the inheritance, Father Jacobs warned me against telling anyone. He said it would attract unscrupulous types who'd only want to marry me because of it; Mother said the same thing."

"So that's what you meant when you said the priest wanted a tithe from you? Has he been trying to get his hands on the money?"

Ann sighed. "He has, and when I wouldn't give him any more, he got Mother involved. Not that she needed much persuading. The reason she doesn't want me to get married is because when I do, she won't be able to get her hands on it anymore." She wiped away a tear that ran down her cheek. "I wish Thomas had never left me the legacy; I don't know who to trust anymore."

Chas struggled to push himself from the bench and hobbled to her. "Come here." He put his arms around her.

"You're safe now. I don't want your money and I won't let anyone take advantage of you. I just want you to be my wife and for us to live at my uncle's house after the wedding."

She nestled into his chest savouring the warmth of his embrace, but suddenly she pulled away. "What about your mother?"

Chas swayed as she moved. "What about her?"

"I heard her say that she wouldn't set foot in a Church of England church and you shouldn't either."

He pulled her close again. "After everything we've been through, do you think I'm going to let that stop us?"

"But I can't get married in a Quaker church. I don't want to turn."

"Then we won't. Do you remember you once said you'd like a clandestine marriage? Well that, my dear, is what you'll get. If you can keep a secret, I'll go and see the bishop tomorrow."

Ann glanced down at his leg. "I don't think you'll be going anywhere tomorrow."

"If it means we can be married, I'll put up with untold pain; besides, I'll be as good as new after a night's rest."

Ann couldn't keep the smile from her face as they walked back from the cathedral to Goswell Road. Once they reached the house, she handed Chas over to the care of Esther, promising to see them both again soon. She turned to leave, but Chas walked with her.

"You will be all right, won't you? With your mother, I mean."

"Yes, I'll be fine. Nothing an extra sixpence a week won't sort out. I'll see you tomorrow."

Ann thought she was floating as she walked down

Compton Street, but she bit down on her lip. *I've got to keep it a secret!* Jane must think we're just friends, for now at least. Her heart fluttered at the thought of seeing Chas again tomorrow. She just needed to work out how she'd meet him, without anyone finding out.

At four o'clock the following afternoon, Ann went into the back yard to check on the washing. As soon as she knew she was alone, she sneaked down the ginnel and out into St John Street. She didn't have to walk far before she heard Chas calling her.

"Over here." He was in a neighbouring alleyway and she hurried over.

"You're here, I was worried you'd be confined to bed." She ran her hand down the side of his face. "It looks a lot better now it's been cleaned up."

"Putting a piece of steak on my eye helped too; you can hardly notice the swelling now."

Ann laughed. "I don't think I'd go so far as to say that. What about your leg?"

"Eve bandaged it up for me; it's bearable and we don't think anything's broken."

"That's a relief."

"And look what I've done today." A grin spread across his face as he took a piece of paper from his pocket. "It's all arranged."

"What's that?"

He showed her the certificate. "Permission from the Bishop of London for us to be married in St James's Church."

"You've been to see the bishop?" Ann's eyes were wide.

His smile twisted. "Not exactly, but there was a clerk who signed it on his behalf. Judging by the people there, I got the impression there are quite a number of these clandestine marriages."

Ann took the letter and traced her finger over his signature. "Is that your writing? It's very smart."

"Smart or not, it means we can be married tomorrow. I've arranged it for ten o'clock."

"Ten o'clock tomorrow!" Her mouth dropped open. "With Father Jacobs?"

Chas sighed. "Yes, that was the tricky bit. He wasn't happy about you embarrassing him yesterday, but I told him there'd be more to come if he refused to marry us."

"I don't suppose he liked that."

Chas grinned. "He didn't but if the bishop's given us permission to marry, who's he to stop us?"

Ann's eyes widened. "What about Mother? He's bound to tell her."

Chas put his hand on her waist. "Not if he wants to keep his reputation intact."

Ann's eyes sparkled. "So you've thought of everything?"

"Oh yes, absolutely everything."

CHAPTER TWENTY-TWO

Forty years later...

Mary leaned forward in her chair. "And so you married him, just like that? Without anyone's permission."

"I did and I don't regret it for a moment." Ann's eyes glistened at the memory. "I put a cross on the marriage certificate alongside his fancy handwriting and we had two witnesses from the church. Mother wasn't happy, of course, but once I promised her two shillings a week for the rest of her life, she softened."

"So you kept in touch with her?"

"I did, and we actually got on better once Father Jacobs left the parish. Apparently, I tarnished his reputation too much for him to stay."

Mary laughed. "I would say it served him right."

"Maybe it did, but Mother wasn't happy that I made her look foolish in front of everyone else either, but we put it behind us for the sake of Jane and Susan. They missed me once I moved out, even though we saw each other most days."

"What about Pa's mother? Did she forgive him for marrying someone who wasn't a Quaker?"

Ann sighed. "It wasn't the fact he married me, but the fact we were married in a church. She never really forgave him for that. When we got home and announced the marriage she was furious. It wasn't helped by the fact that she found out Pa's aunt and uncle had known about it all along, and so she packed her bags and brought the girls back up here with a word. I didn't see them again until years later when we moved back to Birmingham. That was a real shame because we got along very well."

Mary's brow creased. "Why did you move back to Birmingham then, when you had a life in London?"

"That was because of her. We stayed in London for four years and had our first two children while we were at his uncle's house, but then his mother became ill, and with the bankruptcy almost over, Pa decided it was time to make amends."

"Did she forgive you?"

Ann shrugged. "She took a bit of coaxing, but she did in the end, which was important to Pa. Apparently they'd got on well before the bankruptcy."

"What about your family? You must have missed them once you moved here."

Sadness crossed Ann's face. "Mother died the year before we moved and by that time Jane was married and had her own baby daughter. Susan was still only fourteen and so she lived with them until she married six years later. I did miss them, very much, but fortunately, they both married decent men who could read and write, and so we keep in touch by letter. I don't suppose I'd recognise either of them now after all these years."

Mary shuddered as a ghost from her own past was reawakened. "At least you parted on good terms with your family, which is more than I can say about the way my family disowned me."

Ann nodded. "Yes, that was a terrible business."

Mary studied her mother-in-law. "All this explains so much about why you welcomed me into the family so readily."

Ann stared across Mary's shoulder to the window. "I didn't want to see anyone else upset because of religious differences. It makes no sense."

"No, it doesn't."

They sat in amicable silence until Mary turned to Ann once more. "What happened to the money?"

Ann's face lit up. "That turned out to be a godsend."

"So, the creditors didn't get their hands on it?"

"No, we managed to keep it away from them. If you remember, the will had said that once I remarried, I'd take control of the lump sum, but I didn't want to. I spoke to Mr Wood, who said they'd be happy to take care of it until I was ready."

"What did Pa think of that?"

Ann chuckled. "I didn't tell him."

Mary's eyes were wide. "Not at all?"

"Well, he knew I had a bit put to one side, but he had no idea how much, and he said he didn't want to know. He reckoned that if he had anything to do with it, the creditors would think it was his."

Mary grinned. "So he really didn't want you for your money."

"No, he was good to his word. Wood and Sons managed it for me until the bankruptcy was over and then once I passed control to Pa, he bought the house and workshop on Princip Street."

"Really! The house I lived in with Charles that was attached to the brass foundry?" Mary shook her head. "Well I never."

Ann smiled. "It's given us a good living ever since."

Mary cocked her head to one side. "I'm so glad you told me this. Thank you."

Ann folded up her knitting. "I'm glad I told you, too. It's brought back so many memories, but that's not why I did it. I did it because I want you to realise that accepting Mr Wetherby's proposal can be a new beginning for you."

"You think I should accept?"

"I do."

"But you loved Pa; I'm not even sure I like Mr Wetherby. I think of Mr Wetherby in much the same way that you thought of Mr Williams."

Ann shook her head. "No, you don't. I never had any interest in Mr Williams. Our whole relationship was based on the guilt I felt when I first refused to walk out with him. I never wanted to marry him; I just didn't know how to tell him."

"Don't you think I'm like that with Mr Wetherby?"

"No. If you were, this decision wouldn't be tearing you apart. You'd be able to walk away without a backward glance like I did from Mr Williams, but you can't do that, can you?"

Mary hesitated. "I wish I could, but there's just something about him..."

"That something means you care; the problem is you don't love him as much as you loved Charles, but that will change. Mr Wetherby seems to be a genuine man who loves you. There's a lot to be said for that and he's already in a much better position than Pa ever was. You could do a lot worse and if you want a secure future for those children, marrying him must be the best thing to do. I'm sure they'll thank you when they're older."

Thank you for reading *The Young Widow*.
I hope you enjoyed it.

If you did, I'd be delighted if you'd share your thoughts and leave a review.

Just search for VL McBeath on your retailer of choice and scroll to the review section

The *Ambition & Destiny* Series

is a serialised novel inspired by the true story of one family's trials, tribulations and triumphs as they seek their fortune in Victorian-era England.

The full series:

Short Story Prequel: *Condemned by Fate*

Part 1: *Hooks & Eyes*

Part 2: *Less Than Equals*

Part 3: *When Time Runs Out*

Part 4: *Only One Winner*

Part 5: *Different World*

A standalone novel: *The Young Widow*

The full series is available from most good retailers. It is also available in large print on Amazon. To get your copies, search for VL McBeath on your retailers website.

I send out regular newsletters with details of new releases and information relating to the series

By signing up for the newsletter you'll get a FREE digital copy of *Condemned by Fate*.

To get your copy and keep in touch, visit: **www.vlmcbeath.com**

AUTHOR'S NOTE AND ACKNOWLEDGEMENTS

When I finished writing the *Ambition & Destiny* series, I had no plans to add further books. As far I was concerned, the story was over. Over time, however, readers contacted me asking if there would be more.

This got me thinking...

When I initially wrote *Hooks & Eyes*, it contained a lot of backstory that was ultimately removed during editing. One of the deleted scenes related to the fact that Ann had previously been a widow and had then had a whirlwind romance with Chas. I'd always wondered if there was more to this story and so I used the idea as the basis for *The Young Widow*.

I hope the opening to the book shows how the story fits into the main series. To save you having to look, it's a scene that initially sat at the end of chapter twenty-three of *Hooks & Eyes*. At the point, Mary was spending Christmas with the family while she contemplated a marriage proposal. In my early drafts, Ann told Mary her story to show that second chances can have happy endings. It only took a couple of pages but I knew there was room to expand it.

As with the rest of the series, *The Young Widow* was inspired by family history research. It's fair to say, however, that there is more fiction than fact in this story.

What I do know is that Ann was widowed at a very young age. This gave me quite a challenge when researching her past as all I had to go on was her married name, not her maiden name. The fact that her married name was one of the most common surnames in the UK made it almost impossible to trace her. In the end, I had to make a lot of assumptions about her family. None of her family's back story is true although there was a man in the census records for Clerkenwell who could have been her father. With nothing else to go on, I decided that was good enough.

I know a lot more about Chas, although a question I had (and still have) is why he was in London when the rest of the family were in Birmingham. Eventually I decided that he was escaping from the shame of bankruptcy at home.

The storyline about the bankruptcy was true and so it seemed like a plausible explanation. In addition, census records showed that there was a couple in Clerkenwell with the same surname as him. I can't find any evidence to suggest they were related, but the real surname of my paternal ancestors is very unusual, and so I decided it was a good enough connection!

Another part of the story I know to be true is that Chas and his family were Quakers, while Ann was a member of the Church of England. In the early 1800s this probably caused a great deal of family friction. Quakers refused to acknowledge the rituals of the Church of England, such as the marriage service, and many refused to even enter a Church of England establishment. In contrast, those outside the Quaker faith could not have married in a nonconformist church.

Despite that, I know that Ann and Chas were married in Clerkenwell by special licence in a Church of England church. There are several reasons why a couple would do this, but the two I felt were most relevant were:

1) That the couple had different religions or did not attend the parish church because they were nonconformists.

2) The couple faced family opposition to their marriage.

Both seemed plausible and so I used them to help shape the story.

As with all books, I couldn't have done this on my own. I'd like to thank my family and friends for the support they've provided along the way. In particular, I would like to thank my friend Rachel, and husband Stuart for reading early drafts and giving me suggestions as to how it could be improved. I must also thank Susan Cunningham for her editorial work and my advanced review team for final comments.

Finally, will there be any further books in the series?

Possibly.

If you've read the series, you'll know that by the end of *Different World*, I'd tidied up all the loose ends. Having said that, there is the possibility that I could extend the story of Charles and Rose. After the end of the series, I know he went back to sea and I have some evidence to suggest that Rose followed him abroad. Before I can say for sure whether another book is likely, however, I need to do more research to see if I can find any further details of what they got up to ... and why!

If you've signed up for the newsletter, you'll be the first to hear if that book ever becomes a reality.

If you've yet to sign up, you can do so by visiting my website at **www.vlmcbeath.com**.

In addition to joining the mailing list, you'll get a FREE download of the short story prequel, *Condemned by Fate*.

Thank you for reading.

Val

ALSO BY VL MCBEATH

Eliza Thomson Investigates:

A historical cozy murder mysteries series:

A Deadly Tonic (A Novella)

Murder in Moreton

Death of an Honourable Gent

Dying for a Garden Party

A Christmas Murder (A Novella)

A Scottish Fling

For further details visit: **www.vlmcbeath.com**

ABOUT THE AUTHOR

Val started researching her family tree back in 2008. At that time, she had no idea what she would find or where it would lead. By 2010, Val had discovered a story so compelling she was inspired to turn it into a novel. Initially writing for herself, the story grew beyond anything she ever imagined.

Prior to writing, Val trained as a scientist and has worked in the pharmaceutical industry for many years. In 2012, she set up her own consultancy business, and currently splits her time between business and writing.

Born and raised in Liverpool (UK), Val now lives in Cheshire with her husband, youngest daughter and a cat. In addition to family history, her interests include rock music and Liverpool Football Club.

For further information about The *Ambition & Destiny Series*, Victorian History or Val's experiences as she wrote the book, visit her website at: **www.vlmcbeath.com**

FOLLOW ME

at:

Website:
https://valmcbeath.com

Facebook:
https://www.facebook.com/VLMcBeath

Amazon:
https://www.amazon.com/VL-McBeath/e/B01N2TJWEX/

BookBub:
https://www.bookbub.com/authors/vl-mcbeath

Made in the USA
Middletown, DE
01 August 2020

14057553R00125